ENCORE! ENCORE!

"What happened?" asked Clarisse, looking around with apparent surprise. The crowd that had viewed and cheered and laughed with all the acts was almost gone.

"Self-preservation took over," Valentine said, with a grimace. "As soon as the show was over, everybody decided that Slate wasn't the safest place in the world to be, so they went somewhere safer, and more exciting."

"Safe?" Clarisse said with a scowl. "This bar isn't safe? There are five police cruisers parked practically in the front door. District D is less than a hundred feet—"

"I'm talking about murders, Lovelace, not muggings. It's gotten around that the necktie killer hangs out here in Slate...."

"So we spent over a thousand dollars to set up this evening, and everybody leaves five minutes after the show's over. Boy, that's gratitude," Clarisse said softly.

"Not everyone's gone," said Valentine. "The cops are still here."

CANARY

NATHAN ALDYNE

BALLANTINE BOOKS • NEW YORK

Library of Congress Catalog Card Number: 86-90942

ISBN 0-345-33167-2

Manufactured in the United States of America

First Edition: November 1986

**For
Kate Mattes**

part 1

memorial day

chapter one

"UH-OH," DANIEL VALENTINE MUTTERED DARKLY, "AN-other corpse."

"Is my hem straight?" asked Clarisse Lovelace.

Valentine folded his newspaper shut and dropped in onto the highly polished oak table.

Tall and slender, Clarisse stood anxiously before him in the restaurant aisle, wearing a graduation robe as black as her hair. In her right hand she held her gray-tasseled mortarboard and her rolled diploma with a burgundy-colored ribbon tied about it.

"Well?" she urged.

"It's perfect," said Valentine, raising his eyes from the fall of the garment, "but what difference does it make? The ceremony was over half an hour ago."

Clarisse dropped the diploma next to the bowl of fresh sweet william and tossed her mortarboard onto the empty chair next to her. She began unhooking the buttons of her robe. "It made a great deal of difference twenty minutes ago when the class picture was being taken. The photogra-

3

pher insisted on having me in the front row. It was all I could do to smile, I was so worried.''

"Fashion trauma," said Valentine unsympathetically. "Why didn't you just ask the photographer to let you stand in the back row?''

"I did. He said no. I had to be up front. But to make up for it, he asked me out on Wednesday night." She had thrown the robe over the back of the chair and now was straightening the cuffs of her off-white pongee dress. Her hair was fashioned into a flattering but practical page boy that just brushed the nape of her neck. Her eyes were large and dark, and the only makeup she wore was a barely discernible amount of blush and ruby-hued lipstick. She took a cursory glance over the lunchtime crowd at the Atrium, a restaurant located right around the corner from Harvard Square.

"He was just your type, too," Clarisse added as she opened the menu.

Valentine blinked as if he hadn't been paying attention. "Who was my type?''

"The photographer," she replied impatiently, peering into the menu. "He was short, very nicely built, Mediterranean looking, and he had a mustache.''

"Did he ask you to marry him?" Valentine asked absently. "That type always does. Don't bother looking at the menu. I've already ordered for us.''

Clarisse put down the menu and studied her friend. Valentine was gazing past her with a blank, preoccupied stare. He wore a well-tailored poplin suit. His shirt collar was unbuttoned and his wheat-colored tie loosened. His sandy blond hair was trimmed nearly as short as his beard and was as neatly kempt.

Clarisse took up her rolled diploma and tapped one end of it against Valentine's hand. "Why are you so glum?" She waved the diploma before his face. "This is a very big day for me.''

"That wasn't the Nobel Prize they were handing out over there this morning. It was a diploma for a five-day course in bartending.''

4

"I just wanted to get in a little practice at graduating," Clarisse said defensively. "That's all." A couple of weeks before, at the beginning of May, Clarisse had completed her first year at Portia School of Law, located on Mount Vernon Street at the top of Beacon Hill. The day after her last exam, she enrolled in a concentrated bartending course offered by the Harvard Extension School. The skill would enable her to work the afternoon shift and fill in evenings when needed at Slate, the bar Valentine managed in Boston's South End. The added income would provide a wardrobe Clarisse thought befitting a second-year student of corporate law.

The waiter came with a carafe of white wine and two glasses. He poured the wine and then a few moments later returned with a large platter of cheese and fruit. When he had gone away, Clarisse remarked, "You were in high spirits this morning. I could see you in the audience, applauding madly when they called my name. What happened between then and now?"

"I bought the *Globe*."

She bit her lower lip lightly and said, "You mumbled something about a corpse when I came in . . ."

Valentine leaned back and flipped open the paper. "Somebody got his neck gift-wrapped last night."

Clarisse took a sip of her wine, plucked a fresh fig from the platter, and pulled the newspaper about. She turned slightly away from the table, crossed one leg over the other, and rested the open paper on her thigh. She scanned the front page until her eyes stopped in the lower left corner. The headline read:

MAN FOUND STRANGLED
IN SOUTH END
APARTMENT BUILDING

"Barry Pike," she murmured, taking another sip of wine. "Know him?"

"I don't recognize the name."

Clarisse quoted from the article. " '. . . thirty-six years

old . . . unemployed conductor with the B&M Railroad . . . five feet nine inches tall . . .' '' She looked up at Valentine. ''Why do they give his height?'' Valentine shrugged. Clarisse went back to the article. '' '. . . brown hair, mustache, athletic build . . . hands, feet, and neck bound by neckties . . . wearing jeans and a red T-shirt with ''All-American Boy'' printed on it.' '' She looked up. ''Are you sure you don't know him?''

''If they ever make a movie, ninety-five percent of the male population of South End could play the part. Who can tell anything from that? I wish I weren't so bad on names. For all I know, I could have served him five beers a night since the day the bar opened.''

''This doesn't actually say he was gay, does it?''

''Read on. Top of page six.''

Clarisse turned to the continuation of the article. She again read aloud: '' 'Mr. Pike's body was discovered by his roommate, who identified himself only as the victim's ''Significant Other.'' ' '' Clarisse paused to groan, then continued: '' 'The police have ruled out robbery as a possible motive. The victim's roommate confirmed that nothing had been removed from the scene. There was no evidence of forced entry into the apartment, the door of which was found closed but unlocked. According to the medical examiner's report, Mr. Pike had a high level of alcohol in his blood. The examiner also determined there was no physical evidence of sexual activity. The police say they have no suspects at this time.' ''

''When does it say the 'Significant Other' found the body?'' Valentine asked.

Clarisse went back to the inside page. ''Yesterday morning. He'd just come back from a business trip. The medical examiner estimates Mr. Pike had been dead a little more than twenty-four hours.''

''This is Thursday,'' said Valentine thoughtfully. ''He was found on Wednesday morning. Dead for twenty-four hours. So Mr. Pike died early Tuesday morning. Killed by the man he picked up on Monday night.''

Clarisse closed and refolded the newspaper, placing it to

one side of the platter, with the murder headline facedown. "I'll go along with that." Her hand hovered over the platter and finally descended on a small bunch of green grapes. "But I'd like to point out that we're both assuming a trick did it. That might not be the case."

"Give me another scenario, then."

Clarisse shrugged. She couldn't.

Valentine leaned forward and speared a wedge of new peach with his fork. He stared at it for a few moments, then said, "I'm trying to think back to Monday night. I was behind the bar, and we weren't very busy, but I still don't recall a mustached thirty-six-year-old man wearing a red, All-American Boy T-shirt. I think I probably would have. There's something I'm trying to remember, but I can't seem . . ." His voice trailed off.

"Please don't brood about this," interrupted Clarisse. "Your entire purpose in life—for today at least—should be to celebrate my diploma. You should be thinking about how much help I'm going to be to you this summer. Not only will I be your door person, but I will actually be able to fill in when your regular bartenders go on vacation. You won't have to find substitutes. I'll be the best damn bartender you ever saw!"

An hour later, Valentine and Clarisse returned to Boston, alighting from a Cambridge taxi on Warren Avenue in front of Slate. The late-spring afternoon had grown oppressively warm, and the cloudless sky was a brilliant sharp blue. There was no breeze, and a stillness had settled along the avenue. Valentine had removed his tie, and it now spilled out of the breast pocket of his jacket. Clarisse carried her robe over one arm and held her diploma and mortarboard loosely in her other hand.

The building that housed Slate and a similar adjoining structure stood alone on this end of the block. On one side was an abandoned playground frequented by alcoholic vagrants and nocturnal drug addicts. On the other side was the back of the Boston Center for the Arts, a gray and many-windowed complex of buildings running all the way down to Clarendon Street. Directly across Warren Avenue was a line of carefully restored town houses with tall, healthy maples regularly spaced along the sidewalk. These houses took up three-quarters of the block, while the remainder was occupied by the District D police station. Cruisers were parked at an angle on both sides of the street, and double-parked beyond that. Several officers lingered on the main steps of the station house, savoring the warmth of the afternoon. A couple of them waved to Valentine and Clarisse, who waved back before they crossed the sidewalk.

The first floor of the building adjoining Slate was a storefront, now occupied by Peking Video Rental & Sales. The interior of the place was obscured by posters filling the plate-glass windows on either side of the door. The titles were either Chinese kung fu epics or American soft-core erotic films. Posters for the new acquisitions, *Fists of Anger, Fists of Joy,* and *Dixie Does Duluth*, were prominently displayed. Valentine and Clarisse paused a moment to examine the posters before they walked over to the recessed front door of Slate.

The double doors of the bar were propped open, and music poured out of the dim interior. Clarisse cocked her head and listened as Valentine unlocked a small door about ten feet to the right of the bar entrance. Clarisse followed him inside and up the private staircase to the first landing, where they stopped again. Valentine employed a second key to open the door to his private office.

"That song . . ." murmured Clarisse, still grasping for the title as the music grew louder.

Valentine opened the office door. Disgruntled, he said, "What else would you hear playing in a respectable denim-and-leather bar on a warm spring afternoon? It's 'Blue Tango.' "

chapter
two

VALENTINE'S OFFICE WAS COMFORTABLY APPOINTED, WITH an Oriental carpet on the oak floor and two high-backed armchairs raked at an angle toward his desk. Three filing cabinets stood in a corner within easy access. On the wall were several chrome-framed displays of antique playing cards from Valentine's own collection. A second door in the office, directly across from the passage to the stairs, opened onto a narrow iron staircase spiraling down into the barroom coatcheck.

"Seventy-five thousand dollars," said Daniel, grimacing. He went over to the two-way mirror that overlooked the barroom just beneath the office.

Clarisse came up beside him and gazed down into Slate. On the tile floor in the back, a man and a woman were dancing elegantly through slowly revolving blue-and-amber circles of light. "Blue Tango" played on.

"I spent seventy-five thousand dollars of your uncle's money to open a new leather bar in Boston," Valentine explained. It was Clarisse's uncle Noah who actually owned the property, the bar, and the liquor license, but he had moved to Morocco and left the entire management of the operation to Valentine in exchange for a share of the profits. As part of the deal, Valentine and Clarisse lived rent-free in the apartments on the upper two floors. "And what do we get for all that money and work? A racially balanced, bisexual married couple performing period dancing."

The woman executing an elaborate dip at that moment was Niobe Feng, Slate's day bartender. She was dancing with her husband. "But they're not bisexual," Clarisse remarked thoughtfully.

"Niobe likes men, and so does her husband. If that's not bisexual, then I don't know what is."

"It's just the eighties, that's all," Clarisse mused.

Valentine slipped off his jacket and hooked it onto the coat tree by the door. "As long as Niobe has abandoned her post, why don't we go downstairs and you can serve up your first drink as an official substitute purveyor of liquid refreshment."

"Deal," said Clarisse excitedly. "Just let me get rid of these things." She put down the diploma and went up to her apartment with her robe and mortarboard. Clarisse occupied the floor-through at the top of the building, while Valentine had just consolidated for himself the two small apartments on the second floor, directly above the bar and office.

While waiting for Clarisse to return, Valentine sat down in his swivel desk chair. He yawned and leaned back, swinging his feet up onto the corner of the desk and crossing them at the ankles. He hooked his hands behind his head. The tango faded into a rock version of a waltz. Valentine hadn't any doubt that Niobe and her husband continued to dance. He stared up at the ceiling, and after a few moments his expression sobered.

Clarisse returned to the office wearing a loose-fitting white linen blouse, jeans, and sandals. She stopped before the desk. "I'm ready," she said confidently. Then, catching sight of his expression, she demanded, "Are you brooding again?"

Valentine shook his head and sat up. "I just keep thinking there's something I ought to remember about that man who got murdered . . ."

"Come on, let's go downstairs and jog your memory with a drink."

He agreed, and they went down the spiral staircase, through the empty coat check, and into the barroom.

The room had high-ceilings, and a long mahogany bar on the right-hand side. Above the six-foot wainscoting, all four walls were covered with sheets of smooth slate rising to the moulding of the patterned tin ceiling. Two square pillars with a shelf bolted between them divided the room. In the back were an antique telephone booth, an ice machine, rest rooms, and a door that led to a small kitchen. Three globe-and-fan lights as well as track lighting provided illumination.

The low lights made the room dim and cool. At one end of the bar two men sat nursing beers and earnest conversation. One of them paused long enough in his talking to nod to Valentine as he and Clarisse walked past. He looked at Clarisse carefully, and not approvingly. He wore a business suit with his tie loosened. He was one of the shortest men of drinking age Clarisse had ever seen. His shoes dangled eighteen inches above the bar footrest. A third man sat on a stool against the far wall next to the unplugged jukebox. He swayed slightly in time with the music—a chacha now—and watched with a half smile as Niobe and her husband floated in and out of the semidarkness at the back of the room.

Valentine slid up onto a stool at the end of the bar near the ice machine. With a broad proprietary smile, Clarisse ducked beneath the counter and came up behind the bar. She retrieved a roll of clear tape from behind the old-fashioned ornate cash register and tore off two strips. She untied her diploma and used the tape to secure it to the wall next to a black-and-white photograph of herself and Valentine taken the previous New Year's Day at the official opening of Slate.

Clarisse admired her diploma a moment before turning

11

back to Valentine. She placed her hands on the mahogany bar and said, "You look like you've had a hard day, buddy. A stiff belt ought to make you feel better. Name your poison, fella. Dubonnet Fizz? Passion Daiquiri? Sherry Flip? Widow's Slap?"

"A Miller."

Clarisse frowned. She pulled a bottle from the cooler and snapped off the cap. Foam sprayed across Valentine's hand as she slid it across to him. He caught it deftly and toasted her as he raised the beer to his mouth.

Valentine reached into his pocket, withdrew a handful of change, and slid it across the bar in a little heap. "Inaugurate your tip glass."

Clarisse rummaged around on the shelf below the bar for the largest beer mug she could find. She noisily dropped the coins inside, one by one. When she looked up at Valentine, his eyes were wide with surprise.

"The man in the Fenway last December!" he exclaimed.

"What?"

"Strangled with his own belt! Then, on Easter Sunday, a man who got killed on Commonwealth Avenue!"

"No," she said calmly, "I did not commit those murders. I'm sure of it. I have a splendid memory for capital crimes."

Valentine rapped his fist against the bar. "*That's* what I've been trying to remember." He took a swallow of his beer.

"I don't remember the one on Comm Ave. Was he strangled, too?"

"Panty hose," said Valentine smugly.

Clarisse raised an eyebrow.

"He had a female roommate," Valentine explained. "See the pattern? Three gay men strangled with whatever was nearest at hand. A belt. Panty hose. Necktie."

"Robbery?" Clarisse asked.

"Not on Comm Ave. Nothing taken. On the Fenway, I don't remember."

Clarisse's brow furrowed. "Do you think the police have

made the connection? Three gay men strangled in six months?''

"Somebody at *Gay Community News* will point it out to 'em," said Valentine. "Then *Bay Windows* and the *Mirror* will print editorials cautioning against panic in the community.''

The recorded cha-cha crescendoed. Valentine and Clarisse looked over as Niobe and her husband ended their dance with a flourish. The two men at the end of the bar and the man by the jukebox applauded briefly as the couple walked over and slid up onto stools on either side of Valentine. Niobe was slightly winded, not so much from the exertion as from the fact that her clothes were so tight it was impossible for her to take a deep breath.

Niobe was Chinese, large boned and solidly built but not heavy. Her thick black hair was discreetly greased and spiked. She wore a black, low-cut, snugly fitting leotard top and a short black-and-white checked skirt, white hose, and black kung-fu slippers with white embroidery. Beneath her leotard her breasts were hiked up by a stiff old-fashioned brassiere with nose-cone cups. Whatever Niobe wore, she always gave the impression of being trussed.

Niobe's husband was short and slender. His name was Ricky Newton, which everyone who knew him shortened to "Newt." He and Niobe had been married for four years, three and a half of which they had spent apart in a legal separation. Their proceedings for divorce had become so extended and complicated that they had become friends again in trying to sort out the matter. Also, in that time, Newt had come out of the closet, and it was through one of his new gay friends that Niobe had gotten the job at Slate. Niobe Feng had retained her maiden name for esthetic rather then political reasons—she couldn't imagine allowing the name Niobe Newton to be imprinted on her checks.

"A Pearl Harbor, please," Niobe said. Her voice was low and breathy. "And Newt wants a Whiskey Sour." Niobe reached inside her leotard top and violently yanked at the right strap of her brassiere. On Valentine's other

13

side, Newt wore a pair of green army fatigues and a starched tan shirt with epaulets, open to the sternum to display a hairy, tightly muscular chest. He was handsome, with short, wavy black hair, dark eyes, and a beard kept at the five-o'clock-shadow stage.

When Clarisse delivered their drinks, Niobe grabbed her glass and angled it toward Clarisse. "Congratulations!" she said, then added with a rush, "Welcome to the wonderful world of long, thankless hours, lousy tips, inadequate pay, and an endless flow of slurred sob stories."

Valentine drew back. "I pay you well!" he exclaimed, though not angrily. "The customers slap down everything but their lives for you. It's your own fault if you let men slobber their life stories down the front of your dress. And while we're on this, what other employer would let you take dancing lessons on the job?"

"Newt came all the way across town to teach me two new steps," said Niobe, quite obviously changing the drift. "Wasn't that sweet?"

"Very sweet," said Clarisse.

"How are things in Cellulite City?" Valentine asked Newt. Niobe's husband was employed as an instructor of aerobic ballroom dancing at the Universal Woman's Health Spa in Government Center.

"If my girls ever heard you say that, Daniel, they'd come over here *en masse* and practice their Urban Street Defense moves on your head."

"Oh, you're teaching that now, too?" Clarisse said.

"Sure," said Newt, sipping his drink. "It's your basic knee-in-the-groin, eye-gouging, Adam's-apple-crushing stuff. For the up-and-coming professional woman who is tired of being raped in garbage-filled alleyways."

"The All-American Boy could have used some of those moves," Niobe said with a sigh. "I'm gonna miss him. He was my four-thirty regular."

"We were gonna go dancing at Chaps on Sunday night," mused Newt. "Date called on account of death."

Valentine and Clarisse exchanged glances.

Clarisse asked, "Who are you two talking about?"

"Mr. Pike," Valentine said.

"Yes," Newt said. "Barry Pike."

"I never did know his name." said Niobe. "I always called him All-American Boy. That's where he bought all his clothes."

"He was a regular in here?" asked Valentine in surprise.

"Regular isn't the word," said Niobe. "In at four-thirty, out at six-thirty. Wait'll you start working Happy Hour," she groaned to Clarisse. "Remind me to show you how to administer a Vodka IV."

"So that's why I haven't been able to place him," said Valentine. "He was always gone by the time I came on duty."

"When did you last see him?" asked Clarisse.

"This is Thursday," Niobe said thoughtfully. "I didn't see him yesterday. Monday or Tuesday, I guess."

"According to the paper, he was killed Monday night," said Valentine.

"Very late Monday night," Newt said emphatically.

"How do you know that?" asked Valentine.

"Because I spoke to him at two A.M. Monday night— that's actually Tuesday morning, I guess. Right out there in front of the bar. We made a date for the weekend. I was probably the last person to see him alive."

"Except for the guy who killed him," Niobe pointed out.

"Then he *was* in here that night?" Valentine said, perplexed. "But I still don't remember a man in an All-American Boy T-Shirt—especially not one who stayed till last call."

"I didn't say he had been in here," Newt said. "I said I saw him outside here. He told me he was meeting somebody."

"Who makes a date for two o'clock in the morning?" put in Clarisse, coming back from providing more beers to the men down at the other end of the bar.

"When you're unemployed," said Niobe, "time is irrelevant. People make dates at two o'clock in the morning all the time. If they didn't, this bar would be out of busi-

15

ness. However," she went on severely, glancing at her husband, "men separated from their wives who should be working hard and saving up for substantial alimony payments have no business prowling the streets in the middle of the night, making dates with potential murder victims."

"Niobe, by the time our divorce comes through, I'll be mailing your alimony payments to the Golden Lotus Nursing Home for Decrepit Chinese Divorcées."

"Why a necktie?" Clarisse wondered aloud. "Why not a gun or a knife?"

"A necktie is a perfect murder weapon," said Valentine. "Everybody has a tie at home, on the closet door or on their bureau. The murderer doesn't have to worry about carrying a concealed weapon around with him. The victim provides the weapon."

"Same goes for belts, too," Niobe added. "In case a victim doesn't happen to wear neckties."

"True," Newt agreed, and finished his drink in one swallow. He edged off his stool. "I better get back to the health spa. The All-American Boy is dead. What a depressing thought! Good luck, Clarisse—you'll need it if you're going to work with the scourge of the Orient here."

Niobe swiped a clawed hand at Newt but missed. He said his final farewells and left the bar.

"Why does this sort of thing have to happen just when I'm starting to work here?" Clarisse asked Valentine and Niobe. "Now every time I serve a man a drink, I'll wonder if he's a potential victim."

"Or murderer," Valentine said quietly.

"Whatever," said Niobe. "As long as they tip."

At that moment, Clarisse was called away by a man who had just come into the bar. She served him, and while making change at the register, another man carrying several long and slender cylinders of rolled paper entered Slate. He paused briefly on the threshold to remove his sunglasses and allow his eyes to adjust to the dim interior. He was short and slender, with auburn hair. His blue T-shirt intensified his dark tan. A folded softball glove was nestled up under his arm, and a gray patch with a stylized script *S* adorned the cap that was pushed back on his head. He crossed the bar and stopped just behind Valentine.

"I wouldn't advise sliding into home plate in that get-up," said the man.

Valentine looked up into the bar mirror at Jed Black's reflection, then said with apprehension, "You're not going to tell me I forgot about practice? Is it this afternoon? I thought it was tomorrow."

"We moved it up—" Jed looked at Niobe. "I called and left a message yesterday afternoon."

"Uh-oh," said Niobe, "I forgot to bring up the Jim Beam."

"I'll get it," Clarisse volunteered. "How many bottles do we need?"

"I like going down in the cellar." Niobe slipped off the stool, rushed to the back of the bar, lifted the trap door by its massive iron ring, and descended the steep, narrow wooden stairs to the storeroom.

"Anyway," said Jed, "the practice game is today."

In summer, each gay bar in Boston formed its own softball team, made up of staff, staff's friends, and bar regulars. The teams play in heated competition against each other as well as against teams representing bars and other organizations all over New England. Besides the complex schedule of regular games, the league had two weeks of play-offs for the New England championship. The first game of this current season was scheduled for the following weekend, at which time Slate was pitted against the team from Buddies.

"I knew you'd forget," Jed went on. He glanced at the clock behind the bar. "We've got twenty-five minutes. Ten minutes for you to change. Ten to walk me by my office to drop off these plans." He tapped the rolled papers. Jed was an architect with a firm specializing in hospital design. "And five to get to the Common on time."

"Did you forget about practice again?" asked Clarisse, coming up to them.

"It won't take me ten minutes to change," Valentine

said, getting up. He crossed the room and disappeared up the spiral stairs.

"Jed," Clarisse said, "that exotic tan looks suspiciously real to me. But please tell me it's Tan-o-rama. Don't tell me it's—"

"Maui," Jed cut in with malicious pleasure. "I was there for ten days consulting on a community health clinic. How are you?"

"Pale and jealous."

"Come out in the sun, then. Watch us practice. We could use a little cheering on."

"I'm working here now." Clarisse pointed to her diploma taped on the wall. "As of today, I am one of your friendly neighborhood barkeeps. All tips acknowledged with a smile or your next drink free."

"Diet Pepsi," he said, reaching for his wallet.

She waved away his hand. "No, we have an iron-clad policy against charging members of the house team for drinks on the afternoon before a practice." She popped the top on his Pepsi, then discussed the question of whether Hawaii really was the Valhalla of the middle class. Valentine came down. He had changed into running shoes, gray running pants, and a long-sleeved jersey with a gray number twenty-three on it. His cap matched Jed's. He was also carrying a bookkeeping ledger under his arm.

"Clarisse," he said, "If you don't mind, I'd like you to work the first couple of hours of my shift tonight."

"Sure," she began excitedly; then her eyes opened wide. "Wait—tonight's Raffle Night! I can't do Raffle Night on my first day! It'll be a madhouse in here tonight."

"I know, but I have to see the accountant for a few hours right after practice." Clarisse looked about to protest, but Valentine said, "This is your employer speaking. Besides, you'll be fine. I should be back by nine-thirty or ten. Raffle Night's not all that bad, and you know how you love giving out prizes. Besides, we probably won't get more than two or three hundred in here tonight."

"Two or three hundred?!" Clarisse protested, but Valentine was already on his way out the door with Jed.

Alone behind the bar, she glanced with some regret at her diploma. Then she noticed for the first time that the Harvard Extension School had spelled *Clarissse* with three *s*'s.

chapter three

"TIME FOR ME TO GO," SAID NIOBE NONCHALANTLY AS she struggled into a paper-thin black nylon jacket three sizes too small for her. Clarisse glanced around the bar. At the eight o'clock change of shift, there were no more than fifteen customers scattered over the place. A few of the after work crowd lingered, others nursed beers till the prices went down later in the evening, and still others tried unsuccessfully to cruise the first two groups.

"And now that you've learned how to handle a trickle crowd," Niobe went on, "you won't have any problem—"

"Trickle? Good God, at five o'clock on the dot three dozen men surged through those front doors. I had to put up a barbed-wire barricade to keep them from lunging for the bottles on the house shelf. It was—" She broke off suddenly. "What do you do about your feet, Niobe?"

Niobe glanced down. "For one thing, I don't wear heels to work behind here. I dress sensibly." She drew in her breath hard so she'd be able to catch the jacket's zipper.

"Kung-fu slippers are best—they're flat and comfortable. So, I'm leaving now—good luck on your first outing here."

"Wait a minute—you're leaving me alone?"

"Sean'll be here. He's sometimes a little late. But it won't start getting busy till ten, so you should be all right."

Clarisse was left alone in Slate. She had shut the outside doors so as not to attract insects. She had changed the tape three times and now couldn't find any more reels that hadn't been played through. More customers were starting to arrive than were leaving, and still no Sean to back her up. She smiled, . . . made change, . . . opened beers, . . . mixed vokda and tonics, and sliced a dozen lemons and two dozen limes, and—by nine o'clock—began to wonder whether it wouldn't be a good idea to take up smoking again.

Sean arrived an hour late with profuse apologies, with more profuse congratulations for Clarisse's diploma, and with great excitement that she was taking Valentine's place for the evening. He'd brought with him a reel of numbered orange tickets. One was given with each drink bought, and five times in the course of the evening a matching number was drawn from a roll bin behind the bar. In a deal with a theater chain and two gay-owned restaurants in the neighborhood, Slate gave away five prizes of a two-for-one film and dinner coupon. It had always been his ambition, Sean said, to work Raffle Night with a beautiful woman.

"Has it been bad here?" he asked as he rewound the tape she had put on less than a half hour before.

"Not at all," said Clarisse. "The masked gunman's Saturday night special fortunately didn't go off. The explosions turned out to be in the next block. And the ambulance was here in minutes for those two men who had simultaneous heart attacks."

"Tips are always better on nights when there's a little action."

There were too many people wanting drinks for Clarisse to carry on any lengthy conversation with Sean. She continued to fill orders. Sean continued to fiddle with the tape machine. He punched buttons, and adjusted dials, ran the tape backward and forward, stroked the sides of the machine lovingly, peered up at the speakers attached to the ceiling, and at last—music.

Sean Alexander was of medium height, with the sleek muscularity of a gymnast. His complexion was ruddy, and his hazel eyes were deep-set. His smile was sudden and dazzling and frequent. Valentine had hired him nearly four months before, and though Sean worked full-time for Slate, he considered his work behind the bar as merely supplementary income. His real work was making reel-to-reel recordings of music for many Boston bars, both gay and straight. His Back Bay apartment, with its profusion of equipment and stacks of records and tapes, was more like a recording studio than a habitation. He made the tapes for Slate but didn't charge, because he used the crowds to test certain mixes and to watch and solicit reactions.

After ten minutes, Clarisse turned to find Sean with his arms crossed, watching her as he leaned back against a cooler.

"Is something wrong?" she asked.

"No. Thanks for covering me. My clock stopped, and I didn't realize it was so late." He angled his head toward the revolving tapes. "What do you think?"

Clarisse listened a moment and then nodded. "What could I possibly say? Your tapes are *always* fabulous."

"Why do you look so worried, then?" asked Sean.

"I'm thinking about handling the raffle crowd. I did fine with the trickle crowd this afternoon—"

"Trickle?"

Proud of her grasp of the jargon, she explained, "Trickle in, trickle out—" At the moment a group of five men, laughing and talking together, banged through he doors and headed toward the bar.

"Well," said Sean, "relax. Think of Raffle Night as the trickle crowd on speed and it'll give you a handle. Don't worry, all you really have to know is how to open a bottle of Miller Lite."

The five men reached the bar. A mustached man with red hair leaned toward Clarisse and said in a rush, "Vodka on the rocks with a twist, a Harvey Wallbanger, a Piña Colada, two Black Russians, beer chasers all round, three bags of potato chips''—he slapped a twenty down on the bar and smiled—''and change for the cigarette machine, please.''

Clarisse glared at Sean over her shoulder as she reached for a glass.

By ten-thirty, Slate was filled well beyond its legal capacity. Sean had turned on the air-conditioning system, and the stream of cooling air lazily stirred the smoke lacing through the beams of soft amber-and-blue lights.

As Clarisse called out the second winning number of the evening, Valentine returned to the bar. He had on the outfit he'd worn to the practice game. She spotted him as he stood talking to Felix, the runner who sat at the door, collecting the one-dollar cover. When Valentine came over, she met him at the far end of the bar by the ice machine and pointedly flattened both her hands on the counter flap when he reached to lift it.

He looked at her questioningly. "What's wrong?"

"You look haggard. Fatigued. Like you won't make it through the rest of the evening."

"I'm fine. Practice invigorated me." He went to lift the panel again, and again Clarisse resisted.

"Felix is tired," she said. "Why don't you take his place on the door for a while? Let him take a break."

"Why don't *you* sit on the door?" he countered.

Clarisse said nothing. Valentine eyed her with greater suspicion. "You've been getting good tips, right? You want some more, don't you?"

"All right. I admit it. I'm possessed by stark avarice this evening—and I like it. I love picking up wet quarters off the bar and sticking them in my tip glass."

"Okay," Valentine relented, "for tonight, then. But at two-twenty you're going to have to help toss out the dead drunk and the semicomatose."

Clarisse accepted the terms of the bargain. She mixed Valentine a vodka and tonic and then watched as he wound his way through the crowd to relieve Felix at the door.

23

Clarisse was barraged by a flurry of orders and kept busy sliding them across the damp bar. Frequently she collided with Sean as they made change at the middle register. Finally there was a pause in the orders. She poured herself a very weak bourbon and water and was about to take a sip when a deep voice called out from somewhere to her right.

"Scotch on the rocks, please." The "please" was sarcastic, and the voice as a whole seemed forced into a lower register.

Clarisse looked down the bar in that direction but saw no one signaling to her. Everyone along the bar had a drink in hand and was either cruising or talking to a neighbor. She shrugged and took a swallow of her bourbon. The voice came again, louder, lower, and more sarcastic.

"Is this a work stoppage, or are you in a coma?"

Clarisse put her drink down on the cash-register shelf and moved along the bar. At the very end she stopped and peered over the counter flap. He was sandwiched between two tall men with his arms resting on the bar, and so short Clarisse at first thought he might be on his knees. He wasn't. He wore a black leather motorcycle jacket over a white T-shirt with a black eagle stenciled on it. A strip of rawhide was tied around his neck into a single knot against his Adam's apple. He wore a black cowboy hat so large that it increased his height by a good twenty-five percent. The hair showing beneath the hat was a shade of brown darker than the mustache whipping across his thin upper lip. His eyes were masked by silver-lensed aviator glasses.

"What'll it be?" Clarisse asked politely.

"A man could dehydrate in here," he said accusingly. "This would be a great place to hold AA meetings."

"Do you want something to drink?" asked Clarisse. "The Dwarf Toss Competition is not for another half hour."

"A double scotch on the rocks. I'd appreciate it if you *didn't* use a house brand, and try to ease up on the ice, okay?"

Clarisse grabbed a handful of ice, tossed one cube into a glass, and flung the rest back into the cooler. She took a

24

bottle of Cutty Sark from the top shelf and poured the drink. When she'd turned around again, the man was gone. Putting the glass down, Clarisse leaned forward and peered over the bar. The man was hunkered down, retrieving a bill from the inside of his black engineer's boot. The already thick sole and heel of his boots were elevated with at least an inch of additional rubber. The man stood up and wordlessly thrust a crisp ten-dollar bill at her.

When Clarisse brought back his change, he pocketed it all and then asked over the rim of glass, "Where's the regular guy who works here? I can't believe the management is allowing a woman to work behind the bar."

"The 'regular guy,' " Clarisse answered evenly, "is sitting on the door tonight. If you'd looked up when you walked in, you'd have gotten a perfect view of his knee-caps."

The man's mouth curled up in a smirk.

"What's your name?" Clarisse asked.

"Why?"

"Just wondering."

"It's Mike. Wondering what?"

Clarisse leaned forward, arms folded on the bar. "Wondering if anybody ever tried to eat peanuts off the top of your head."

Grimacing, Mike pushed his dark glasses up on the bridge of his nose with a stab of his index finger. Able to see his entire face, Clarisse realized he was the same short man she'd seen in the bar that afternoon. He hadn't looked at her in any friendly way then, either.

Clarisse leaned back up and started slightly. Standing directly behind Mike was a trio clad head to foot in black leather—two men and a woman between them. The men wore matching outfits—many-zippered motorcycle jackets, buttoned vests over bare chests, leather pants with even more zippers than the jackets, wide silver-studded belts, and black boots. Confederate-style hats were pulled low over their brows, and like Mike, the two men wore silvered aviator glasses. The man to the right of the woman was taking measured puffs on a large black cigar jammed into his mouth. In one hand he held a slack leash attached to a studded dog collar fitting around his dress-alike's neck.

The woman between the men had longish honey-blonde hair in soft waves brushed back from her finely featured face. Her eyes were dark and deep set, and she wore no makeup. Her body was lithe and voluptuous, her breasts cupped in black leather with straps encircling her shoulders, crossing her midrift and disappearing into low-slung leather pants. Tight thick bands of leather bound her toned biceps and wrists. One gold stud earring sparkled in her left ear.

The man holding the leash looked over at the woman and asked, "What'll it be, B.J.?"

"Jack Daniels." She addressed Clarisse in a surprisingly soft voice. "Straight up."

"And two Heinekens," the leash holder added as he fished bills out of a zippered jacket pocket. The three of them came forward a step and hemmed Mike in.

The man on the leash looked down at Mike and asked curiously, "How tall are you, anyway?"

In the mirror, Mike had eyed the trio with interest. His look of appreciation faded. "Tall enough to chew your balls off without standing on my toes," he snapped.

The woman, B.J., reached over and patted Mike on top of his hat with an indulgent smile. "Now, now," she said. Giving him no further notice, the trio took their drinks and moved to the back of the bar.

"Boston's swarming with rude people," Mike growled to Clarisse. "Not like in Los Angeles."

"Is that where you're from?"

He nodded. "People in L.A. are crazy, but they're polite."

"Perhaps if you sheathed that honed tongue of yours—" Clarisse began gently.

"If I want a lecture," said Mike, cutting her off, "I'll call my lover."

Clarisse dipped her hand into her tip glass and slapped a dime onto the bar. "Phone booth's in the back."

Mike pushed the coin back. "We broke up," he said sullenly.

"I'm not surprised to hear it," returned Clarisse.

"It was his fault," said Mike.

Clarisse moved away to accommodate a clutch of men at the far end of the bar, and when she came back, she was surprised to find Mike still there. "It really was his fault," Mike told her, and added accusingly, "He's the one who started cooking, not me."

"He was a lousy cook?"

"No! He's a terrific cook. He stopped going out to the bars just so he could save money to buy a pasta maker and this machine that makes sherbet—I hate sherbet—and a microwave, and you wouldn't believe what other junk like that. He'd fix all this food, and then he'd get mad because I wouldn't help him eat it. All he thinks about is his stomach. He used to be sexy, but after a while it was like having an affair with the Pillsbury Dough Boy. I want somebody to take care of all of me—not just my stomach. You know what I mean?"

"Sure," Sean shot over Clarisse's shoulder as he made change at the cash register. "We all want somebody to take care of us."

"I mean emotionally," Mike said.

"That, too," Sean said with a wink, and hurried away.

"You know," said Mike, angling a thumb toward Sean, "he's hot. Everytime I see him, he looks hotter."

"So tell him," said Clarisse. "I know for a fact he can't cook."

"It wouldn't do me any good telling him. He already knows it. All I ever get from him is attitude."

"Well," spoke a masculine voice, "maybe one day when Sean finds himself knee-deep in your drool, he'll speak to you." Niobe's husband, Newt, had angled into the bar at Mike's side.

Scowling at Newt from under his hat, Mike took his drink and waded out into the crowd.

Newt greeted Clarisse with a smile. "I'll have a Becks."

Clarisse refused his money as she handed him his beer.

"You know him? Mike? He was hanging around telling me stories about his ex. In his sullen, sarcastic way I think he was trying to be friendly."

Newt grunted. "I wouldn't trust that one to tie his shoelaces without an ulterior motive." Thanking Clarisse again for the beer, Newt squeezed through the crowd back toward the door. There Valentine was perched on a high stool, taking up the dollar cover and greeting the evening's patrons. Leaning against the wall next to Valentine in the recessed doorway was Jed Black, cane in one hand and an enormous padded brace on his right foot.

"Did your dog bite you again?" Newt asked.

"You got a dog?" Valentine asked. "When?"

"I'm referring to the Ice Maiden," Newt explained.

"He means my roommate," said Jed. "I fell off some scaffolding this afternoon." He tapped his cane against his padded foot. "Looks worse than it is."

"And if you don't mind," added Valentine to Newt, "you'll be playing shortstop on Saturday."

"You bet," Newt said. "Hey, Jed, if you're really injured, maybe I can be first-string for the rest of the season."

"Not a chance," said Jed. "This is two weeks tops."

"Newt," said Valentine, "tell me what you know about that leather trio standing in the back. Two men and a woman."

"The Four Horsemen of the Apocalypse minus one," Newt smirked, without even having to turn around to look.

"Just tell me what you know," said Valentine.

"Not much, really. The one with the cigar is called Ruder. The one on the leash is Cruder. The woman's B.J."

"What are their real names?" Jed asked.

"Who knows?" Newt said. "Who cares?"

Valentine watched the three as B.J. carefully looked over the crowd, sized men up, and made comments to her escorts. Hardly a man who came near escaped their scrupulous review.

"I know I haven't seen her before," Valentine said. "But the two men . . . I can't tell with those glasses on."

"Those two have been around *for-ev-er*," Newt groaned. "They live in New Hampshire and drive down every Thursday, Friday, and Saturday night. Without fail. They think Boston is the Big City. They bought all that leather gear through a mail-order catalog. Ruder slings chintz. Cruder is a show clipper."

"What?" asked Jed.

"Ruder is a decorator," Newt explained. "Cruder grooms poodles—" Newt took a breath and then added with high disapproval, "in their kitchen."

"And the woman?" Valentine asked.

"Went to school in Boston. Used to be arrow straight. Then she moved to New Jersey and discovered leather, heavy drugs, and gay men—all in one night. Now she's into *The Outer Limits*."

"What does she do during the day?" Valentine asked.

"She hangs out in a tunnel with two hundred humpy men . . ."

Both Valentine and Jed looked at him questioningly.

"She's an urban archaeologist. On loan from the state of New Jersey. She's working on the subway extension in Cambridge. It's B.J.'s job to make sure they don't destroy anything of archaeological importance."

"For somebody who doesn't know much about them," said Jed, "you know a lot."

Newt shrugged. "I've talked to them," he said vaguely. From the door Valentine watched the trio in the back of the bar. Mike had managed to get beside them. They looked the short man over, B.J. commenting to the men openly about him and obtaining from them nods of approval. She spoke to Mike, and Mike responded eagerly.

"I guess Mike's the Fourth Horseman for the evening," said Newt, who'd been watching, as well.

"Is that Famine?" asked Valentine. "Or War?"

"Pestilence," said Jed.

"No," Newt said, shaking his head, "the Fourth Horseman was Death."

chapter
four

"WHA . . . ?" VALENTINE SAID AS HE LOWERED HIS COF-
fee mug. He leaned across the table, squinting his eyes
slightly.

Clarisse sat oposite him, obscured behind the open arts
section of the *Boston Globe* as she sipped her coffee. The
rest of the paper lay scattered over the floor around her
chair. A plate of Danish and almond squares was set on
the table between them.

It was Sunday morning of Memorial Day weekend, and
Valentine and Clarisse were sitting in the kitchen of his
apartment. There had originally been two apartments on
the second floor of the building, but when the other tenants
moved out, Valentine converted the two units into a floor-
through. Now only he, and Clarisse on the floor above,
lived in the building. Valentine's apartment was casually
laid out and decorated. From his bed, peculiarly angled in
the large room at the front of the apartment, he had a perfect view into the policemen's locker room in the District
D station. His back windows, in the kitchen, looked out to
a portion of the deserted playground, Tremont Street be-

yond that, and an impressive view of a portion of the Boston skyline.

" 'Wha . . . ?' *what*?" Clarisse asked blearily, not putting down the paper.

"An advertisement for an all-female production of *Death of a Salesman*." Valentine lightly flicked the newspaper with his forefinger. "This is one evening in the theater I don't think we ought to miss," he said, and sat back.

Clarisse lowered the paper and then flipped it over toward herself. She read the advertisement upside down. "I forgot to tell you," she said groggily, "I already ordered tickets." She yawned involuntarily.

"You look awful," Valentine commented. He ignored her frown and took a sip of his coffee.

Clarisse crumpled the newspaper as she closed it and slapped it onto the table. "Valentine, that is the third time this morning that you've told me how bad I look"—her eyes flicked to a clock on the shelf over the stove—"and it's only ten-thirty!"

"You're cranky, too," he added. He broke off a large piece of raspberry Danish and dropped it on his plate. Clarisse claimed the remaining half. She reached over and took the pot of coffee from the automatic maker, poured herself a fresh mug, and refreshed Daniel's. "I never should have gone to bartenders' school," she complained. "I should have taken summer courses at Portia. Then I wouldn't be sitting here looking as terrible as I feel."

"I warned you not to swill while you're working behind the bar."

Clarisse gave him a look of mortal offense. "I had a few cocktails toward the end of the evening. I did not *swill*. Besides, last night was the second double shift I've worked in three days. Why is it you never ask Niobe to fill in for you? She always looks fine the next morning, no matter what she did the night before."

"Because I hired you to work double shift when it's necessary."

"Why are you so mean to me this morning?" She demanded.

31

Valentine rapped the knuckles of one hand against his baseball cap, knocking it slightly back on his head. "Pre-game jitters, I guess. Sorry." He was wearing his Slate baseball uniform—pin-striped, turn-of-the-century style, with knickers and gray hose. His pitcher's glove rested on the table next to the coffee maker.

Clarisse stared blankly out the window at the derelict brick playhouse in the playground. When she finished her Danish, she turned to Valentine.

"It's killing me that I can't go to the game today," she said. She leaned forward, resting her forearms on the table. "Val, why couldn't I open the bar a little later? Just today. It wouldn't make that much difference, and I'd cheer my-self hoarse for you at the game."

"Can't do that," Valentine said. "Think of yourself as a sports widow and you'll feel better."

Clarisse made no reply, but cocked her head toward the main apartment door between the kitchen and the living room. "Someone's coming up." Valentine made a move to rise but didn't even make it out of his chair before the apartment door was flung wide.

Niobe Feng, wearing a crimson outfit with crimson patent-leather shoes with gray laces, made a bounding leap into the kitchen. She wildly shook two enormous red-and-gray pom-poms above her head, which was adorned with crimson bows. With savage gusto she chanted:

RAH! RAH! SIS BOOM BAH!
KICK 'EM IN THEIR NUTS!
PUNCH 'EM IN THEIR GUTS!
SLICE 'EM, DICE 'EM,
FILLET 'EM AND PUREE 'EM!
GO-OOOOO, TEAM! GO-OOOOO, TEAM!

"Well, what do you think?" she demanded, beaming a smile at Valentine and Clarisse. She shook out her pom-poms, and a few stray strips of colored paper drifted down onto the remaining Danish. "That's the new Slate softball-team cheer," she explained. She draped the pom-poms over the back of one chair and pulled up another to the table.

"It certainly gets the message across," Valentine ventured after a moment.

Instead of sitting down, Niobe rushed back to the open door. Stepping onto the outer landing for a moment, she returned carrying a folded tabloid-sized newspaper and a small wooden box. The box was gray and red with a brass handle screwed into the top. "Newt and I worked out that cheer last night. We practiced it all night long." She closed the door and crossed to the table, placing the paper and box down before she sat.

"Your neighbors must have been delighted," Clarisse remarked.

"They're afraid of me," Niobe returned, shrugging. She leaned across the table and peered closely at Clarisse. "You look just terrible."

As if taking that as a cue, Valentine got up quickly and busied himself with getting coffee and a plate for Niobe.

"I worked a double again yesterday so that this one"— she cocked a thumb in Valentine's direction—"could go out on a hot date."

"Was it busy last night?" Niobe asked sympathetically.

"It was a nightmare," Clarisse said huskily. "I jammed the tape machine and ruined Sean's new tape. Seven cases of empty beer bottles fell on top of me. A pair of lovers barricaded themselves in the ladies' room and had a violent breakup—for an hour and a half—at the top of their lungs, until Sean finally got the door off the hinges and threw them out. At a quarter to two, when I was dragging the trash out to the side of the building, a bum in the playground spilled Sterno all over himself and caught on fire. He was wearing sixteen layers of clothing, so the fire department got there before the fire got down to his skin. Sean, of course, invited the firemen inside for coffee, which I ended up making, because Sean was too busy trying to pick up one of the firemen who was going off duty. He succeeded, so I had to clean up all by myself. I didn't get to bed till after four o'clock."

33

"Little annoyances come with the territory," Valentine said loftily.

Niobe delicately wiped away crumbs from her mouth. "Wait'll you work a full moon," she said.

Clarisse made a little hissing noise. "I should know better than to expect sympathy from either of you."

"How do you like my outfit?" Niobe broke in. "Newt designed it, and I sewed what I couldn't buy."

"It's very . . . eye-catching," Clarisse said diplomatically.

Niobe narrowed her slanted eyes. "You hate it! I can tell by your tone!"

"I don't hate it, Niobe. It's . . . well—"

"What? What?"

"Snug," Clarisse finished. "I mean, with all the jumping up and down you'll be doing, it doesn't look as if it's going to be comfortable."

"I like my clothes to fit," said Niobe defensively. "The worst feeling in the world is having material slipping and sliding all over my body. Gives me the willies. I like to know that something's not going to fall off while I'm walking down the street."

During this, Valentine sat down again and peered speculatively at the gray-and-red box Niobe had brought in with her. It was the size of a small shoe box, with ornate brass wirework covering three inch-square openings on either side. A miniature brass padlock dangled from an ornate latch. "This is a very peculiar purse, Niobe."

"It's not a purse," Niobe said. "It's a mascot."

Wiping the crumbs from her hands, Niobe smartly slapped the top of the box. From inside erupted a shrieking blast of angry chirps, accompanied by a furious scratching against the wire. Two sharp yellow claws and a bit of puffy yellow feather shot out through one of the wire grates. The whole box rocked on the tabletop. "It's a canary," she told them.

Valentine and Clarisse glanced at one another. Valentine leaned down cautiously to peer inside.

Without asking permission, Niobe got up and opened the

refrigerator. She looked about inside and took out a small plastic container of leftover meat loaf and returned to the table.

"Valentine!" she yelled, yanking the cage over to her place. "Stop making faces at him! You'll make him sick!"

"Did you give it a name yet?" Valentine asked.

"Rodan."

"As in Japanese monster movies?" Clarisse asked.

Niobe took a bit of the cold meat loaf with her fingers and pushed it through the grating. "Here's breakfast, baby," she cooed.

"It's carnivorous?" Valentine asked incredulously. "It's a carnivorous canary?"

Niobe nodded and pushed more meat inside the cage. "The man at the pet shop told me it goes wild over fresh kielbasa, but I think that's too greasy, don't you?"

The cheerleader then sat up and looked at both their empty plates. "You two done eating?" Without waiting for a reply, she flipped open the *Herald* she'd brought with her.

Niobe folded the paper carefully into quarters and then held it up for them to see. "Do you recognize this person?" she asked, waving the paper first toward Valentine and then toward Clarisse. She held up a photograph of a clean-shaven young man in a business suit. The caption was concealed by her hand.

"Are we supposed to know him?" Valentine inquired.

"Wait, wait." Niobe turned the paper away from them. "Do you have a pen?"

Valentine leaned back and retrieved a felt-tip pen from a counter drawer. With it Niobe made rapid short strokes on the photograph. When she clicked the pen shut, she flipped the paper back around again. "Now do you recognize him?" she demanded.

Niobe had added a thin mustache and a large hat.

"That shrimp in the cowboy hat!" Clarisse exclaimed without hesitation. "The one who gave me such a hard time last Thursday night."

"Valentine?" Niobe said.

"His name's Mike," said Valentine, troubled. "Why is his picture in the paper?"

Niobe lifted two fingers, and the bottom of the page dropped down into view. Clarisse's expression darkened. "Oh, no," she said.

Beneath the photograph the headline read: "Police Link Fourth Gay Killing to Necktie Murderer."

Niobe relinquished the paper to Clarisse. She crumbled more meat loaf through the wire mesh of Rodan's cage as Clarisse read the article aloud. Valentine's mouth creased into a tight frown as he listened. He'd put on his baseball glove and was prodding the supple leather with his closed fingertips.

"Almost exactly like the last murder," Clarisse said when she finished. "Bound with his own neckties. No sign of robbery. No indication of sexual activity. Dead at least twenty-four hours and discovered by a friend."

Valentine slammed his glove angrily onto the table. Rodan squawked in protest. "At least twenty-four hours," he repeated bitterly. "Do you know what that means?"

Niobe looked up. "That in this weather he was a pretty ripe corpse?"

Valentine shook his head. "Body found late Saturday morning, dead twenty-four hours. Since Friday morning, which probably means he got killed by whoever took him home on Thursday night. And where did Clarisse say he was on Thursday night? At Slate."

"I can't believe this is happening," Clarisse said, peering at the photograph. "I served him drinks. I listened to his trials and tribulations. And now he's dead?"

Niobe grimaced. "If you two are going to break out the black crepe over that dwarf, I'm getting out of here."

"You knew him, too?" Valentine asked her.

"I bounced his little buns out of the bar one afternoon a couple of months ago."

"Why?" asked Clarisse.

"He was giving me a hard time," said Niobe simply.

"Whoever is killing all these people is as good as invisible," Valentine said.

"I'll bet the killer is clean shaven," Niobe speculated. "Nice looking, average." She screwed her face into a sour expression. "Who's going to remember a man like that? People remember beards and mustaches. I'll bet he's well built too, because he subdues his victims."

"Niobe," Clarisse said, "the shrimp couldn't have been more than four foot two, and he was thin. He couldn't have fought his way out of a Roach Motel."

"Oh, yeah," Niobe conceded, then after a moment of thought, said, "but All-American Boy *wasn't*. He lifted weights and belonged to the gym, but he ended up tied to his bed."

Clarisse looked at Valentine. "You were on the door Thursday night. Did you see him leave with anybody?"

Valentine thought for a moment. "No. For a while he was talking to those two leatherettes who were with that peculiar woman, but nothing came of it. He left by himself, so far as I can remember. About one-thirty."

"This is depressing," Clarisse said. "I don't need this with the way I feel already today."

"I know just what you mean," Niobe said with no emotional backup in her tone. "I'm all broken up inside." she glanced at the clock. "Daniel, we have to get a move on. Warm-up is eleven sharp."

Clarisse pushed her chair back from the table. "I think I'll go for a walk. It'll make me feel better. Mind if I tag along with you two as far as Copley Square?"

"I know what that means," Valentine said, standing. "You're going to make a beeline to Copley Place. Whenever you get depressed, you go shopping."

"Through some major clerical error," said Clarisse, "Neiman-Marcus sent me a charge card. I intend to run it up to my limit before they check my credit rating and realize what a mistake they've made."

Niobe snatched up the bird cage and held it to her face. "We're gonna lead our boys to victory with cheers and

37

chirps, aren't we, Rodan?'' She shook the bird cage and was satisfied only when the bird squawked and fluttered madly against the walls of its cage.

chapter
five

VALENTINE WIPED THE BACK OF HIS LEFT HAND ACROSS his forehead, erasing an irritating trickle of sweat. He looked up through squinted eyes. The early-afternoon sky was darkened by thick charcoal-gray clouds, and the scent of impending rain was strong in the humid air. The storm had been predicted for the night before, but Boston weathermen were famed for their habitual inaccuracy. Valentine firmly wrapped his palms around the bat he'd been weighing in his right hand. He turned his attention to the pitcher's mound and prodded the earth with one cleated foot before taking his position and raising the bat to his shoulder.

He was standing at home plate on the municipal diamond on the Charles Street side of the Boston Common. From where he stood, Valentine had a clear view of the lush Public Garden across the street and the traffic streaming toward Beacon Hill.

The game was going into the sixth inning. Slate was pitted against the team from the Eagle this Memorial Day weekend, and the Eagle had been winning until Sean Alexander slammed a home run on a two-ball, no-strike pitch to even the score. Valentine hoped to break that tie and keep Slate ahead until the game was over. He glanced to his left. The tiny crowd in the bleachers—not to mention his own team—evidently found his turn at bat to be of less interest than the heated argument being pursued by Newt and Niobe, at the top of their voices. Niobe was swinging Rodan's tiny cage back and forth with more than a vague sense of threat. Tiny tufts of yellow feather spat out of the cage's air vents.

"Heads up," the catcher hunkering behind Valentine warned.

Valentine turned his concentration back to the pitcher— a tall, clean-shaven man with wavy hair who was one of the acting managers of the Eagle.

With a slight nod of his head, Valentine indicated that he was ready. The pitcher performed an elaborate windup, thrust forward, and sailed the ball toward the home plate.

The ball thudded into Valentine's stomach.

Valentine groaned and let go of the bat. He pitched violently forward, throwing out his right hand to break his fall. Three of his fingers bent far back as he hit the hard-packed earth.

Valentine rolled onto his side, coiling into a fetal position and yelping as he tried to figure out which hurt more— his stomach or his hand. Niobe and Newt collided with each other racing to get to home plate.

"Water!" screamed Niobe, going to her knees on the ground next to Valentine. "Get me water!"

Someone thrust a half-empty bottle of Perrier at her, and she immediately upended it over Valentine's head. As the spring water splashed over his face, he expelled his breath in a single groaning blast. A wedge of squeezed lime popped out of the bottle and grazed off his cheek.

"It was an accident!" the pitcher pleaded. "I swear it was an accident!" He went to his knees at Valentine's side next to Niobe.

"Shall I call an ambulance?" Newt asked.

Valentine struggled to sit up, but Niobe immediately

pushed him back onto the ground. "Stay put until I can figure out if you're going to live." She took his injured hand into hers and turned it gently palm up. Valentine yelped. "There goes the ball game," Niobe muttered with a doleful shake of her head. She looked up at the faces ranged in a circle around her. "Broken," she said factually, then added less positively, "I think."

"Oh, God, Val," the pitcher moaned, "I didn't mean to break your finger."

"You're a vicious beast!" Niobe snapped at the man. "You deliberately tossed a knuckleball, and you know it. I saw you."

"You weren't watching me," the pitcher shot back heatedly. "You were fighting with Newt. As per usual," he added with a sarcastic grimace.

"I see everything!" She snapped her fingers at the man's face. "Knuckleballs can fly wild, and they're dangerous unless you're a professional, which you obviously are not!"

Valentine wrested himself out of Niobe's grip and came to a sitting position. Through gritted teeth he said, "It was an accident, and while you two have been arguing this thing out, I have been sitting here suffering. Sean, Niobe, help me up."

As they were hoisting Valentine to his feet, a raindrop splashed against his cheek, and thunder rumbled ominously in the near distance. Valentine looked at the distressed pitcher. "If you'll drive me over to New England Medical, I won't sue." The hospital was only a few blocks from the Common.

"I'm just parked on Charles," the pitcher said.

"We'll all go," Newt declared. The Slate team chimed in with firm agreement.

Valentine shook his head. "If all of you want to be a help," he began just as rain began to fall in a light misty shower, "go over to Sailor's. I'll meet you there when I get done at the hospital and give you the damage report."

Sailor's was a bar on Boylston Street just across from the Common. The drab, whitewashed exterior of the place could be seen from where they stood.

Thunder crashed overhead, and the mist of rain changed without warning into a sheeting downpour.

"Go on!" Valentine shouted. "I don't want those new uniforms to shrink!"

The Eagle pitcher, again apologizing profusely, rushed with Valentine down the slope of ground. They darted through traffic to his car on the other side of the street. The Eagle team and the two dozen sodden spectators dispersed in various directions, while the Slate team, gathering bats, balls, and mitts, rushed *en masse* across Boylston Street and then clamored through the door into the dim, cool, red-lighted interior of Sailor's.

VALENTINE JOINED THE TEAM AN HOUR AND A HALF later. Aside from the ballplayers who had gathered around the pool table, only a few customers were scattered throughout the bar at this early hour. Sailor's was a hustler bar. Valentine noted that on this rainy Saturday afternoon the avarice and energy seemed at a low ebb, with the half-dozen hustlers basking about in the red light, waiting for the advances of the johns slumped in the shadows. Valentine walked up to the long bar in the back and ordered a beer from a middle-aged bartender with bright bleached hair and an artificial tan. He slid two bills across to the man and picked up the sweating can of Miller in his un-injured hand. The two middle fingers of Valentine's right hand were bound together and held stiff by a splint. He made his way over to the pool table where Niobe was pitted against Newt. It was a long moment before anyone realized Valentine was there, but when Niobe looked up and saw him, she flung her pool cue in Sean's general direction and rushed over.

The remaining team members—the shortstop and one of the outfielders had gone home—gathered around, asking Valentine a hundred questions at once. Valentine could tell by the number of empty cans spread about that the thirst created by the aborted game must have been thoroughly quenched by now.

"All right, you guys!" Niobe yelled. "Put a lid on it!" Everyone went silent.

"It's a bad sprain. Nothing's broken," said Valentine. "But this hand'll be out of commission for a while—and I'll be off the team for the rest of the season."

"*What* season?" said Sean, swallowing off the remainder of his beer. "With you *and* Jed out of the lineup, we're not going to have a *chance* at the play-offs . . ."

"I'm going over to see Jed," said Valentine. "When he sees this hand, maybe he won't feel so bad."

"It's still raining out," said Sean. "Stay and have a beer."

"Yeah," said Newt, "you got to catch up with us."

"He couldn't," snapped Niobe. "You've had six in the past hour. It's four o'clock in the afternoon, and you're ossified."

"I was just trying to keep up with you," returned Newt. "I never could."

"Rain makes me melancholy," Niobe explained. "And if I weren't afraid of denting this fake diamond engagement ring you foisted off on me, I'd knock your face off right here and now."

"Okay, you two, don't start," Valentine warned. "I'm still going over to see Jed, rain or no rain. I talked to him yesterday, and he sounded pretty down."

"We'll all go," said Niobe expansively, having already forgotten the quarrel with her ex-husband. "We all need cheering up."

The team began to herd out of the bar. Sean lingered behind a moment with Valentine.

"Are we sure that Jed is going to welcome a drunk softball team showing up unannounced on his doorstep?"

Valentine nodded. "It's all right. He told me yesterday I should bring the team over after the game."

Sean shrugged and smiled, tapping the brim of his cap. "You're the captain."

"Not anymore," said Valentine. "Not with this hand." He snatched Sean's hat off his head and replaced it with his own. "You're team captain now."

OUTSIDE, THE RAIN HAD STOPPED. CLOUDS HAD TORN apart, revealing wide patches of blue sky. The humidity had abated, and the air was cooler. The Slate team strolled down Charles Street, with Valentine and Niobe in the lead. Niobe was swinging Rodan's cage in a wide arc.

Jed lived in a spacious building on Mount Vernon Street between Charles and West Cedar. The team crowded the wide stoop, and Valentine depressed the buzzer for the fourth-floor apartment. A few seconds later a garbled voice rasped through the intercom speaker. Valentine announced himself, and the voice replied with another incomprehensible mutter before snapping off. Niobe peered through one of the side strips of glass at each side of the door.

"Ahh," she announced after a few moments, "the Ice Maiden cometh."

The main door was pulled open to reveal Jed Black's roommate, Press. He frowned slightly when he saw the number of callers. "Well, well, if it isn't Spanky and Our Gang." Press had a pale but not unhealthy complexion, pure platinum hair worn in a longish slash cut, piercing blue eyes, and a drooping platinum mustache. His blue work shirt and jeans were streaked with paint. His feet were bare. Press's manner, under almost all circumstances, was fairly chilled, and Niobe wasn't the only one who referred to him as the Ice Maiden.

"Miss Manners maintains that civility is in this year, Press," Niobe said.

The blond man tightened his mouth into a smile and then dropped the expression immediately. "How was that?"

"Enchanting," Niobe said.

"We dropped by to see Jed," Valentine explained.

Press drew a breath and released it with a hissing sound. "I thought you'd want to come inside. I suppose it wouldn't do any good if I told you I think Jed's napping."

"No good at all," Newt put in from farther down the stoop.

Press peered through at Newt. "You're drunk." He

swept his eyes appraisingly over the rest of them. "In fact, I think you're all drunk."

"Val's not," said Niobe. "But he's injured. Show Press your hand, Val. Now let us in before I make a scene on your doorstep."

"Before?" echoed Press skeptically, stepping aside. "All of you look like you've just made a mass escape from the detox ward."

As the Slate team filed in, Valentine automatically headed toward the elevator at the back of the entrance hall, but Press waved him away from it.

"Elevator's out," he said, starting up the staircase. "Follow me—if you're not all too drunk to hold on to the banister, that is."

"I *am not* drunk!" Niobe screamed.

"You're plowed," said Newt, right behind her, poking her sides playfully.

On his way up, Press looked over his shoulder at Valentine. "What happened to your hand? You pick up some rough trade?"

"Game injury," Valentine said shortly.

"Injuries on the ballfield, deaths in the barroom," Press sing-songed as they crossed the second landing. "You ought to put a sign up over the door of Slate—'Abandon Hope All Ye Who Enter Here.' "

"Press, you have wit as well as good looks," Niobe said sarcastically.

"I hear," Press said, "that the county coroner is about to open a branch office next door to your bar. You're providing so much of their business nowadays."

"Sic 'im, Rodan," Newt said, joggling the canary's cage.

Upon reaching the fourth-floor landing, the team gathered outside the door of Press and Jed's apartment. Niobe, wheezing dramatically, fell against the wall. "I'm exhausted! I hate climbing stairs! Whose idiotic idea was this, anyway?"

Press opened the apartment door and led the team into the living room. Sunlight poured in through two high win-

dows overlooking Mount Vernon Street. In one corner a
color television was turned on at low volume, showing
hordes of frightened people fleeing before an angry dino-
saur crashing through Times Square. To the right of the
main door was an archway leading to a wide, short hallway
with three closed doors. In one corner of the living room
the rug had been thrown far back and furniture moved
away. There a metal easel supported a large rectangular
canvas. The painting bore a portrait of Jed Black standing
against a wintry view of the Public Garden. Press had evidently been interrupted in his work on the painting, for he
strolled back over to the easel and picked up his palette
and brush from a table scattered with tubes of paint.

After stacking their equipment as much out of the way
as possible, the team gathered around the easel and voiced
their admiration while the others looked at Press's framed
work on the living-room walls. Most of the members of
the team had never visited Jed's apartment before, though
they knew Press, or at least had spoken to him.

The third baseman was staring at three charcoal portraits
hung one atop the other between the two large windows.
He pointed to the middle picture. "Hey, this one's you,
Daniel." He looked down at the lower portrait, didn't recognize the model, and brought his eyes up to the drawing
above Valentine's likeness. "Isn't that—!" He broke off,
taking a closer look at the image.

"God!" exclaimed Niobe, poking her head into the small
kitchen. "Don't you guys ever do your dishes? There's a
culture field in your sink."

"Are you people here to visit Jed or take inventory?"
Press asked without looking up from his work.

"I didn't know you had done a portrait of me," said
Valentine, looking over at the charcoal drawing. He was
very pleased—Press's picture showed him what he had always felt he *wanted* to look like. "When did you do that?"

"I did it from memory," Press explained vaguely. "And
Jed had a photograph of you. You have an interesting face.
In certain lights."

"Is there one of me?" Niobe inquired, looking eagerly about the room.

"It's in that room," Press replied, pointing at an open door at the very end of the hall. "Right above the toilet."

"Ha-ha," Niobe said, and then her eye caught the charcoal portrait directly above Valentine's likeness. "That's All-American Boy!" she cried, pointing.

"I knew he looked familiar," said the third baseman complacently. "I knew it was somebody who was dead, but I just couldn't remember who exactly."

"Who else is in here?" Niobe asked excitedly, going from one portrait to the next all around the room. "Who else—"

She stopped suddenly at a small square ink drawing of a man wearing a cowboy hat that was much too large for him.

"It's the Shrimp!" she exclaimed. "My God, Press, your walls are covered with dead people."

All eyes turned questioningly to Press. He dismissed them with a frowning glare over his shoulder. "I do faces I find interesting, that's all. If the Slate killer has the same taste that I do, it's hardly my fault."

"Don't call him the 'Slate killer,' " Valentine snapped.

" 'A rose by any other . . .' " Press mused.

Niobe rapidly completed her circuit inventory of the pictures in the room.

"No more dead people," she concluded finally. "It is pretty weird, though, Press."

"I thought you people came over to visit Jed," Press said angrily, slapping his brush onto the table and turning to face the group.

"You said he was asleep," said Valentine.

"Yes," said Press, "Jed can sleep through anything—which he's just proved. Valentine," he added with a meaningful smile, "you know where his bedroom is. And you all have to answer to him for the cleat marks on his newly polished floors."

"All right," Niobe said in an exaggerated whisper.

"Where's Rodan? We're going to give Jed a real rouser of a cheer—"

Niobe, Newt, and the rest of the team crept quietly behind Valentine as he walked down the hallway toward the door of Jed's bedroom. He stopped at one side of the bedroom door and leaned sideways to grasp the knob. He waited as Niobe fluffed her pom-poms and then held them in position as she readied herself into a spring-squat that would propel her into the room. She affixed a broad smile to her face and nodded a go-ahead to Valentine.

Valentine wrenched at the knob and flung the door open wide. He pulled back out of Niobe's way as she flew past him, screaming:

RAH! RAH! SIS BOO—OH, MY GOD!

Valentine thrust his head into Jed's bedroom.

Niobe had landed with a thud at Jed's bedside. Jed was sitting up against the headboard, staring at her. Two neckties were tightly bound around his neck, their ends tied about either side of the headboard. His legs were folded beneath his haunches, ankles bound by two ties attached to a third, securing his arms behind his back. Except for the bright bands of silk and wool—and a blue bandanna stuffed deep into his mouth—Jed was naked. His cane had been placed on the bed, the end of it pointing between his legs.

chapter
six

"DAMN!" CLARISSE CRIED AS THE BLADE OF THE PARING knife sliced a shallow groove across her thumb. She flung the knife onto the butcher-block table and rushed over to the roll of paper towels mounted above the aluminum sink. She swathed the blue paper tightly about her thumb, but not quickly enough to keep blood from dribbling down the bib of her white apron.

At the cutting table Niobe paused to ask, "How bad is it?" before smashing apart a head of lettuce. Newt was beside her, rapidly slicing cucumbers. They both had on white aprons, but Niobe also wore a paper hat, now resting precariously atop her spiked hair. The table was covered with a bounty of fresh raw vegetables intended for an enormous aluminum salad bowl in the middle of the table.

The kitchen, located just off the Slate barroom, was a small but conveniently laid out space. It was put to full use only on Sundays, when Slate, like the other gay bars in the city, offered a very reasonably priced buffet to its customers. Around town, these buffets were staggered so that it was possible for the very hungry or the very sociable to hit five or six in succession. Slate's brunch, at one P.M., came first. Valentine and Clarisse had prepared the food the first few times, until Niobe mentioned Newt's culinary expertise and he was hired for the weekly event. The buffets were popular and proved a successful way to take up the slack of a slow Sunday afternoon.

"I don't think it's too bad," Clarisse said, and lifted the paper to look. Blood gushed from the wound, and she wrapped the towel once more around her thumb.

"You cut your finger because you're distracted and depressed about Jed," said Niobe confidently.

"Of course I'm depressed and distracted. I'd feel worse if I weren't upset about it."

"Think how I must feel," said Niobe, adjusting the strap of her brassiere where it was biting into the flesh of her shoulder. "I was the one who found him." She picked a slice of vegetable from the salad bowl. "His face was as purple as this beet." She popped the beet slice sadly into her mouth.

"That's the problem with people when they die," Newt added as he scraped the cucumber into a pile. "They're suddenly the center of attention"—he looked up and waved his knife at Clarisse—"whether they deserve it or not. Don't get me wrong. Jed was great, but no matter how many flowers we send, he's still not going to smell them."

"You're so damned sensitive, Newt," Niobe observed as she wrenched apart a head of Romaine. "I guess that's why I married you."

"I don't believe you two!" Clarisse cried. In her frustration she grabbed a handful of carved radishes and flung them into the salad bowl. "You're being positively and totally callous about this."

Newt and Niobe looked up at her, exchanged glances with one another, and went back to their work.

Angered further that neither Newt nor Niobe would defend their attitude, Clarisse tore off another square of paper toweling and loosely rebound her finger, securing the improvised bandage with a rubber band.

"I'm going to start putting things out." Clarisse sullenly

picked up a large container of knives, forks, and spoons and piled two economy-size packs of paper napkins atop it. With a frowning scowl of disapproval for Niobe and Newt, both of whom avoided her gaze, she backed out the single swinging door into the barroom.

A long white linen covered table was set up in the open back area. Plates and saucers were stacked on one end of the table, and a large arrangement of daisies, a gift from a florist friend of Valentine's, was prominently displayed mid-table. Steam trays were already in place, although the Sterno heaters were not yet lit. Clarisse placed the tray of flatware down next to the plates and then crossed to turn on the tape machine. As the music filled the bar, she went about arranging several rows of paper napkins on the table. Earlier, she and Niobe had brought up cases of liquor and beer from the cellar and refilled the ice chest behind the bar.

When she finished with the table, Clarisse removed her apron and tossed it on a shelf behind the bar. She looked in the mirror to right a wayward strand of her dark hair and then frowned unhappily at her reflection. Worry and a fitful night's sleep had taken their toll about her eyes, despite an attempt to disguise her condition with makeup. Clarisse sighed, came around the bar, and walked to the front doors.

After propping open the inside set of doors, she unbolted the two heavy main doors, then gripped the handles in both hands. She yanked the doors inward, shutting her eyes against the blast of bright sunlight. When she opened them again, a black-clad man was standing directly in front of her. His appearance there was so sudden and startling that Clarisse gasped in alarm. Her hands tightened on the door handles, ready to slam them shut again if need be. Yet her grip relaxed when her eyes adjusted to the change of light and she saw the small rectangle of white just below the man's prominent Adam's apple. He was wearing a clerical collar.

Clarisse, startled again, looked the priest over. He was only a little taller than she, with reddish-blond hair and blue eyes. His complexion was pinkish and even this early in the season had proved its inability to take the sun. Clarisse guessed he might be near forty, but it was hard to tell his age any closer than that. It was much easier to discern a fondness for alcohol in his puffy cheeks and his red-tipped nose.

"Good afternoon," she greeted him uncertainly.

"You're late opening today," he said.

"Just a bit." Clarisse secured the doors open and then faced the priest again.

"I'm sorry I startled you like that," he apologized.

"It's all right. Umm, are you here to see the manager?"

"No, I'm here to have a drink."

Clarisse hesitated a brief moment and then said, "You know this is a gay bar . . ."

"Yes, in fact I do. If you're not prejudiced against clergy, the clergy would dearly love a gin and tonic."

Clarisse shook her head and went back into the bar, the priest following closely behind her.

"I've been on my feet since six A.M. Two high masses, a christening, and a wedding. The christening was twins. Screamed like hell." The priest sidled up onto a stool near the ice machine as Clarisse ducked behind the bar.

She mixed a generous gin and tonic for the man, and after he had taken a long swallow of it, he presented her with a satisfied smile. He had already laid out two one-dollar bills. Looking around the empty barroom, he asked, "Is Niobe off today?"

"She's in the kitchen, cooking," Clarisse replied, wondering more and more. "There's a brunch today."

"Ah, yes," he said, nodding. "I forgot about that. My name is Father McKimmon. Father *Cornelius* McKimmon. You must be Clarisse. Niobe's mentioned you a few times."

"How well do you know Niobe?" Clarisse inquired curiously. She picked up a fresh bar towel and began to polish glasses.

"Around here, you might say, I'm a semiregular."

"Semiregular?"

"I say mass at the men's shelter on Pine Street every

third Sunday." He took another swallow, finishing off the drink. "Believe me, I need this." He handed the glass back to Clarisse, and she mixed a fresh one. "Besides, this is the one place where I am absolutely safe from the well-intentioned ladies of the Rosary Altar Society."

"The what?"

"Women of the parish who volunteer their time to keep fresh flowers on the church altar, polish the holy instruments, make sure the priests are kept in good cheer, and so forth. Unfortunately, their taste in liquid refreshment hardly ever runs to good gin."

"I see," Clarisse said slowly.

Father McKimmon looked at her a moment. "It bothers you to have me in here, doesn't it?"

"No," Clarisse replied firmly, "It's just— Well . . . I don't think I've ever seen a priest in a bar in broad daylight before—in uniform, so to speak."

"Well, if the Rosaries start looking for me—and I put nothing past them—this is surely one of the last places they'll try."

"Is your parish around here?"

"I'm at the other end of the Orange," he answered cryptically.

"I see," Clarisse said. She would have pursued the matter if a second customer hadn't entered the bar at that moment. He was a tall bearded man who, despite the warmth of the day, was wearing a black leather jacket. He ordered a Budweiser, and as Clarisse snapped off the top, she watched to see if the man showed any surprise at Father McKimmon's presence.

"Corny!" called out the man in the leather jacket. As Clarisse watched with widened eyes, he took his Budweiser down to the far end of the bar and fell into hushed but animated conversation with the priest. Father McKimmon, Clarisse decided, might be more than a semiregular.

When she returned to the kitchen to check on the progress of the preparations for brunch, she found Newt and Niobe standing on opposite sides of the table, glaring at one another.

53

"Are you two throwing vegetables again?" Clarisse demanded. "Last Sunday this whole kitchen was littered with shallots."

"The next thing I throw," Newt muttered, "will have a shiny sharp edge and a wooden handle."

Clarisse leaned against the refrigerator with an exasperated sigh. "Niobe, where is the 'other end of the Orange'? One point five seconds after I opened the front doors today, we got our first customer—a priest."

Niobe glanced up at the calendar taped to the wall next to the sinks. "Oh, yes, it's Father McKimmon's day, isn't it? Every third Sunday of the month, like clockwork." She looked at Clarisse. "Tell Corny I'll be out to see him as soon as I've committed my first capital crime of the day, would you? The other end of the Orange means the subway line. The Orange Line ends in Malden."

"His parish is in Malden?" Clarisse asked.

"Let's put it this way," Newt cut in. "Father McKimmon says mass in Malden, but he hears confession all over Boston—in every gay bar in town."

"Newt!" Niobe cried. "That is not true! You just don't like Corny because he promised me that if I ever converted to Catholicism he'd perform an exorcism on you."

"He's a closet lush!" Newt waved a stalk of celery at Niobe. "You only defend him because he gives you tips on the dogs."

"Is that true, Niobe?" Clarisse asked.

Niobe heaved a loud sigh. "Father McKimmon is not the only priest in the world who plays the dogs at Wonderland. It's no big deal. He *is* a human being, you know."

"What about his vows of chastity and poverty?" Newt challenged. "That doesn't include swilling down liquor in gay bars, picking up lapsed altar boys, and playing the dogs four days a week." Newt leaned far over the table and swept the leaves of the celery stalk back and forth across Niobe's nose. She angrily slapped it out of his hand.

"You know," said Clarisse, "people are going to be upset if all the food we serve is bruised beyond recognition because you two pelted one another with it. Val told me

54

he'd dock you both a day's pay if there were any more complaints this week about blood on the quiche." Clarisse pushed through the door back into the barroom, announcing over her shoulder, "Brunch is served in half an hour."

Father McKimmon had moved to the opposite end of the bar. He was deep in conversation with yet another customer. A half-dozen more men had come in, the man in the leather jacket having joined them. When Clarisse came back behind the bar to take orders, she was surprised to see that the young man with Father McKimmon was Press.

Clarisse served the other customers and then took a bottle of St. Pauli Girl down to Press. The blond young man looked weary, his eyes less alert than usual, and he hadn't shaved. He rubbed a hand over his stubble of beard as he listened to the priest. Clarisse wondered what to say to Press about the death of Jed Black the day before. Everything seemed either inadequate or rude, so she opted for silence.

Yet the concern in Clarisse's eyes was apparent, for Father McKimmon said quietly, "I was just offering my condolences."

Press picked up his beer and angled it first at Clarisse and then at Father McKimmon. "Thank you both," he said in a cold, constrained voice. "Your sympathy is appreciated." He swallowed and put the bottle down with a bang. "But—don't tell me you're shocked. Don't tell me you're horrified. Don't tell me you can't imagine how such a horrible thing could have happened to someone like Jed. And do not ask me for the grisly details. In fact, Father McKimmon, I'd rather not talk about it at all."

"I don't mind, Press," the priest said, "but are you sure it wouldn't help to talk about it?"

"I've never found religion much of a comfort."

"I see," Father McKimmon said quietly. With the mark of his hurt on his face, he slipped off his stool. "I'll see you later." He retreated to the other end of the room.

"He was just trying to be understanding," said Clarisse, piqued.

"In the past twenty-four hours I've been through the

works," Press said wearily. "The last thing I need now is to have banalities and gin breathed in my face by Corny McKimmon."

"You know him?"

"I met him through Jed. Jed was an altar boy when he grew up in Malden."

Clarisse couldn't resist throwing a glance over her shoulder at the priest. "I'd better go away, as well," she said, turning back to Press. "Otherwise, I'll start offering condolences, too."

"Condolences accepted," said Press shortly with a real attempt at graciousness. "I bring you a message from across the street. Daniel said he'd be over as soon as possible."

"You were talking with the cops across the street?" Clarisse asked, surprised. "You live in District A; this is District D."

"After the boys in my district got done, they asked me if I'd come over here to talk with a couple of detectives who've been working on these necktie murders. When I got there, Daniel was waiting in one of the upstairs hallways."

"What did they want to know?" Two more customers came into Slate. They went to the bar, and one of them called down to get Clarisse's attention. "In one second," she called back with an engaging smile, and then immediately returned her attention to Press.

"They asked about Jed, of course, and they asked me a lot about this place."

"This place? Slate, you mean?"

Press watched her as he took a swallow of his beer. He put the bottle down, scratching at the label with his thumbnail. "They're suspicious about this bar," he said without looking up. "They called it 'The Last-Date Dive.' "

"What . . .?"

"According to the detectives I talked with," said Press, "the common factor in these killings is that the murder victims were in Slate before they were killed."

56

"The police are saying Slate is a hangout for murderers?"

"One, anyway. They didn't come right out and point fingers, but they implied things."

"Rumor is a lot more destructive than outright accusation. A rumor like that getting around town could ruin our business."

"Well, then, maybe you ought to schedule your bankruptcy hearing, because the rumor's *already* around town."

"But it's not true. It's just coincidence that those people were in here before they were killed."

Press shrugged. "I'm only telling what I heard."

"We'll just have to start an antirumor campaign."

"Right," said Press. "The way Nixon tried to start an antirumor that the president of the United States wasn't a crook. It doesn't work that way. People want to believe the worst."

"I guess you're right, but I think it stinks. What else did the cops ask you?"

"What do you mean?"

"Like: Why didn't you find Jed's body before the softball team showed up? And: Didn't you think it was odd that Jed didn't come out of his room all day while you were there?"

"First of all, I didn't get back to the apartment until eight-thirty yesterday morning." His tone was defensive. "I was dancing at the Loft all night, which—by the way—I can prove. When I finally got back to the apartment around six-thirty, I assumed Jed was still asleep. I went to bed myself and didn't get up till about half an hour before the damn ball team barged in. I figured Jed had been up and about for hours and had come home to take his regular Saturday afternoon nap. He always rested up before he went out on Saturday night. There was nothing strange about the fact that I hadn't seen him."

"It never occurred to you to knock on his door, to see if he was all right?"

"No, he could have been sleeping. Or with a trick. In our little household, the cardinal rule was 'Open closed

57

bedroom doors only in case of nuclear attack.' Besides,''
Press added after a beat, "Jed and I weren't getting along
too well lately."

"You two had been fighting?"

Press shook his head. "Jed didn't fight. He was the sullen, silent type. So am I. We left notes."

"Things were that bad?"

"We weren't lovers, for Christ's sake," snapped Press.
"We were just roommates, but we'd have been a hell of a
lot happier living alone. Jed didn't want a lover. Neither
do I particularly." Press paused again and added, almost
bitterly, "Unless he's rich and hates Italian food."

"But in the meantime you'll have to find another roommate."

"No," Press said, "I won't."

Clarisse looked at him inquisitively.

"I was Jed's beneficiary. His insurance money comes to
me. All of it. Jed set that up a couple of years ago, when
we were still speaking." He looked suddenly at Clarisse
and evidently read the dismay in her eyes. "I'm still sorry
he's dead."

"Oh, Press," said Clarisse with a trace of grimness in
her smile, "you're just a sentimentalist in your heart of
hearts."

"I'm just realistic," Press said as he slipped off the stool.
"I'm also taking off before the brunch starts. It'll turn into
a wake if I don't. Tell Daniel to call me so we can compare
notes on the third degree."

Press winked at Clarisse and pointedly ignored Father
McKimmon's farewell wave from the other end of the bar.

Clarisse stared after him. Her mouth tightened. She
grabbed up his empty beer bottle, swiped a bar towel across
the mahogany to daub up the rings of dampness, and started
down the bar toward her impatient customers. Instead of
depositing the bottle in the proper case, she flung it hard
into an empty trash container. The green glass shattered
loudly against the metal bottom.

part 2

gay pride day

chapter
seven

"A BLOWJOB?!" SEAN EXCLAIMED IN SHOCK. "THE THEME of our float is going to be a blowjob?"

"No!" Clarisse cried. "A blow-*dryer*."

It was two forty-five in the morning. Boston's Gay Pride parade would start sharp at noon the following day. Parked in front of Slate was a baby Toyota pickup, lent to the bar for the parade by a friend of Sean's. On a wooden platform over the truck bed was mounted a chicken-wire frame that nearly engulfed the small vehicle. Valentine had built the platform, and Niobe and Newt had sculpted the chicken-wire frame into the shape of a hand-held hair dryer. Clarisse had volunteered to stuff the wire with the contents of approximately one hundred and twenty boxes of pastel-colored tissues.

The theme of this year's parade was "Gay Contributions to Modern Culture," and the floats entered by various gay bars were to reflect some aspect of this theme. Chaps had chosen dance; Buddies took music; the Eagle, food; the Ramrod, fashion; and Graystone Bar got literature. Because he had been late for the organizational meeting, Valentine was left no choice but personal grooming for Slate.

Clarisse had wanted to get started earlier but had to wait until after Slate closed because Valentine asked her to take an extra shift.

Clarisse sat on one of the two barricade sawhorses she'd managed to borrow from District D. She looked over the wire frame, which appeared to have enough holes for all one hundred twenty boxes of tissues, and sighed.

"It's a hundred degrees tonight," said Clarisse.

"Ninety-two," said Sean.

"Well, we'd better get started."

"Oh no," Sean said. "*I'm* the one who said I'd get the truck, and *you're* the one who said you'd stuff the tissues."

"You can't do this to me," Clarisse cried, pushing away from the sawhorse.

"It wasn't my bargain—it was yours. And I did my part."

Clarisse started to object but stopped herself. "Okay,' she conceded. "You're right, but why don't you get us a beer and we'll talk about it."

"It would take more than a beer to change my mind, but what kind would you like?"

"A Molson," Clarisse said with resignation.

While Sean was inside the bar, Clarisse opened two dozen boxes of ochre, coral, and tan tissues and set them onto the back of the float. She decided to begin stuffing the body, trigger, and barrel of the blowdryer, which to her eye looked more like a six-shooter than a bathroom appliance. The base of the float would be done in smoke-blue-and-ivory diagonal stripes against an aquamarine background.

Clarisse climbed up onto the platform, but before beginning work, she paused to glance down Warren Avenue. Despite the late hour, and because of the oppressive heat, the area was surprisingly active. A paddy wagon had pulled up in front of the police station and two policemen were rousting a small band of drunken college-age men and women out of the back and herding them inside. A few feet away another policeman was aiding an exotically dressed, coiffed, and handcuffed woman out of the back-seat of a cruiser. In a loud Spanish-accented voice she was likening members of the officer's immediate family to various barnyard animals. Clarisse looked toward Clarendon Street. Lights were still on in several town houses on the other side of the street, and from one of them came Michael Jackson's voice filtering through the thick-leaved maples lining the sidewalk. Clarisse could just make out the shadowy forms of several people reclining on stoops. A male couple ambled along the sidewalk, talking in hushed tones. She had seen them in the bar earlier in the evening, and though she waved, they did not wave back.

Clarisse picked up a box of coral tissues, plucked one out, twisted it into a flower, and tied the stem of the flower around the chicken wire.

"God," said Sean when he reappeared a quarter of an hour later, "I can't believe how hot it is tonight. How's it going?"

Clarisse looked down at Sean's empty hand. "It would go a lot better if I had that beer I asked for."

"Valentine's bringing it out to you. I have to go."

"You're really not going to stay and help?"

"I honestly can't, Clarisse. I've got some tapes to set up for tomorrow night. I'm gonna be working straight through myself."

"Traitor," Clarisse remarked. "Turncoat. Villain."

Valentine ambled out of the bar with her beer. "I told him it was okay," he told her.

"All right, then," said Clarisse, taking the bottle of beer. He carried a Miller Lite for himself. The fingers Valentine had badly sprained weeks earlier had healed sufficiently for the bandage and splint to be removed. He had developed an unconscious habit of flexing his hand to work out the lingering stiffness.

"See you at the rally," Sean said. Waving, he sauntered into the darkness of Warren Avenue on his way toward Clarendon Street.

Clarisse took a swallow of her beer, relaxed, and said, "You and I'll have this done in record time."

"I don't know how to stuff chicken wire," Valentine admitted.

"Don't worry, I'll teach you." Clarisse pulled out a tissue and waved it up toward the light for Valentine to see. "It's the easiest thing in the world."

"Clarisse, may I remind you that you *wanted* to do this part of the job? That you *begged* for it."

Clarisse glumly turned back to the barrel of the blow-dryer. It was about four feet long. "I thought it would be sort of fun," she said glumly. "But I also thought I'd get help doing this."

Valentine shrugged. "I helped. I built the platform."

"You're not even going to keep me company at least?"

"I suppose I could bring a pillow out and sleep on the curb," he offered, "but I have no intention of being awake in the next ten minutes."

"Then go inside," Clarisse said loftily. "Let me work in peace."

"Thank you, Ms. Martyr," said Valentine. "Now that that's settled, I'm going to bed." He looked up at the inky sky as he finished his beer. "It'll be dawn soon enough," he said. "The boys across the street'll come running if you need them."

"Go to bed, Val, before you make me paranoid."

Valentine said a final farewell and went inside by the private door to the right of the bar's entrance.

Alone, Clarisse continued working. Noise abated slightly down the dark street. It was evidently too hot to sleep. Police cars came and went, discharging prisoners. The policemen occasionally wandered over to Clarisse and her float.

"What's it going to be?" one of the cops asked. "What's the theme?"

"Antivivisection," said Clarisse offhandedly.

"Oh, yeah?" said the cop doubtfully. He moved over to view the blow-dryer from a slightly different angle. "At

64

first I thought it might be gun control. The thing looks like a pistol.''

By four A.M. Clarisse had finished with the dryer frame. She climbed down from the float, stepped back a short distance, and looked at it. In the stark sodium light of the street lamp, the colors seemed peculiar and false, but Clarisse assumed that in daylight they would look fabulous. She went inside the bar and brought out another bottle of Molson and a folding chair. She opened the chair and set it in the street next to the truck. She sat down and began on one of the side panels that would eventually read: PERSONAL GROOMING in enormous block letters.

The panel on the back of the truck would spell out SLATE in the script lettering used in all the bar's advertising.

She had finished PERS and was moving her chair twice when she suddenly developed the eerie sensation of being watched. She flicked up her eyes and scanned Warren Avenue. It was deserted now in the last truly dark half hour before dawn, but the feeling seized her more strongly than ever. She twisted about in her chair and drew her breath sharply, a handful of pink tissue fluttering from one hand.

Three faces—B.J. and the men Valentine had told her were nicknamed Ruder and Cruder—stared at her intently. The men wore mirrored sunglasses and were dressed in their usual ill-fitting leather outfits. B.J. wore leather also—pants and a vest buttoned high enough not to disguise her cleavage. In one hand she carried a black leather brassiere, slapping it rhythmically against her thigh.

B.J. waved her brassiere at the wire-and-wood frame extending well up over the cabin of the truck.

"This it?" B.J. asked, disappointed. She shook back her rumpled wavy hair.

"It's not quite finished yet," Clarisse said defensively. "The colors will show up much better in the sunlight."

"We heard somebody was down here building a float in my honor. A seventeen-foot B.J."

"It looks like a gun to me," commented Ruder, at B.J's right.

"I can't tell what it is," Cruder said, "but it sure as hell doesn't look like you, B.J."

"It's a blow-dryer," said Clarisse, exasperated. "Where did you hear this rumor anyway?"

"At a party," said B.J.

"A party? Did Sean Alexander tell it to you? If he left me here with all this work and sneaked off to some party, I'll—"

"Sean?" B.J. interrupted. "That bartender? Cute, clean shaven . . ."

Clarisse nodded.

"Haven't seen him," said B.J. "I'd have remembered it if I came across that one tonight. Especially at this party." B.J. twirled her leather bra about her hand. "It was an intimate affair."

"I got rope burns." Ruder held up his arms, pushing his wrists a couple of inches out of his jacket. "Got 'em on my ankles, too."

"Oh . . ." Clarisse blinked. "I see . . ." She turned back distractedly to the float. "Excuse me, but I have to get this finished."

The sound of rock music erupted from down the street. Both B.J. and her companions swiveled their heads in that direction.

"Sounds like a party," Ruder said vaguely. "Somebody's having a party down there somewhere."

"Let's go find out," Cruder said. "I'm still speeding, anyway."

"Why not?" B.J. added. "It's Saturday now. Who's holding the Quaaludes?"

The trio wandered away into the darkness, and Clarisse worked steadily and uninterrupted for the next two hours. The street grew quieter at last, though the temperature seemed to rise and the air grew more sultry. The sky began to lighten, and the streetlights flickered off. Clarisse could see the colored tissues in natural light. They would have looked wonderful, she decided, if they had not already begun to wilt so badly.

She finally finished the float at eight o'clock and was

suddenly aware of the ringing of a distant bell marking the hour. She took this to be a good omen. Stretching and yawning, she decided she was too tired to climb the stairs to her apartment and did not want to leave the float unattended. Instead, she climbed into the cab of the truck, rolled down the windows, stretched out as best she could across the seat, and fell asleep.

chapter
eight

CLARISSE DIDN'T IMMEDIATELY OPEN HER EYES. AS SHE awoke she tried to figure out where she was. She heard many voices in conversation and laughter. She heard a badly amplified woman's voice singing from a distance. She smelled hot dogs and shish kebab.

Her legs itched badly, and whatever she was lying on was hard and lumpy. As she opened her eyes gradually, she saw green leaves high above her. "Hmm," she said.

"Welcome back," Valentine said.

She turned her head in the direction of his voice. "Oh," she groaned.

"What's the matter?"

Clarisse eased herself up and scooted back slightly to lean against the linden tree next to Valentine. She looked around. They were on the grassy knoll on the Charles Street side of the Boston Common. All about them the Gay Pride Rally was in full swing. From where she sat, Clarisse judged there were fifteen to twenty thousand people. She yawned and stretched, sitting up to arch her back. "I feel rested. How long have I been asleep?'' She dropped her hands into her lap.

"Two hours. It's nearly four o'clock.''

The parade, originating in Copley Square, had wound a couple of miles along Boston's narrow streets, along the same official route the march had taken for the past ten years, before spilling finally into the Common for an afternoon of entertainment and political speeches. Many thousands had lined the streets as cheerers-on, as bemused spectators, or even in some cases as hecklers. The bars' floats were considered a great success. It was led off by Chaps' tribute to dance—a life-sized revolving figure of Michael Jackson with blaring music to back it up. The Eagle float, representing gay culinary achievements—an enormous spinach salad, quiche, and bottle of Perrier water—followed this. One of the more popular floats was the one from Buddies—which had chosen great music. The bartenders of Buddies had constructed an enormous skyline of Oz with a rainbow arched above it. A yellow road led out of Oz, in the middle of which was a slowly turning medallion displaying the profile of Judy Garland as "Over the Rainbow" played repeatedly. Next to last was Greystone's tribute to gay literature—Gertrude Stein and Walt Whitman shaking hands across a lavender ocean. With Clarisse nervously driving the baby Toyota, the engine temperature indicator always hovering in the danger zone, Slate's blow-dryer brought up the rear.

After parking the Toyota truck, Valentine and Clarisse had trudged up the knoll toward the Civil War Memorial and settled themselves beneath the first unoccupied linden they found.

Clarisse got unsteadily to her feet and looked around. "It's still going great guns.''

A large, quiet group of women was gathered on blankets and towels before the bandstand, listening to two very short women singing a duet about walking hand in hand in the rain in Vermont. The AIDS Action Committee hot-air balloon was vainly trying to make another ascension from the softball field—five dollars for a perfect view of Boston.

Moving through the crowd was a well-built, mustachioed man wearing a black half mask, green silk cape, tank top, and green-and-white-striped silk shorts. Bold red lettering across his chest read: Captain Condom. Close beside the captain was a shorter man dressed in flesh-colored spandex and resurrected Hula-Hoops, fashioned into a recognizable likeness of a condom. The two of them together represented a community health clinic with a large gay clientele. As they moved about, they distributed pamphlets on "safe sex."

Many clustered about the dozen stands offering a wide variety of foods from hamburgers and hot dogs to exotic Greek and Eastern fare. Most of the men gave only cursory but longing glances over a table selling homemade desserts but flocked to a stand vending pita pocket bread overflowing with lettuce, fresh meat, and raw vegetables. Since the afternoon was sunny and hot, a lot of men and women simply lay on the grass, picnicked, or milled about. Cameramen and reporters from several television stations were searching for something peculiar or embarrassing to record.

Clarisse got the attention of a woman selling cold cans of Coke and bought two. She unsnapped them both and handed one to Valentine as she sat down again.

"Stop looking at those two Italian muscle boys, Val," she said. "Looking isn't getting."

"Speak for yourself," he said as he took the cola from her. "I already got a wink from the little one and a nasty glare from his friend." He took a swallow and pushed himself nearer Clarisse.

All of the entered floats, except the one from Slate, were parked on the far side of the softball-field grandstand facing toward the knoll. The Slate entry was parked on Charles Street. The large hair dryer was now no more than a piled tangle of twisted chicken wire and tissues, looking as if a small bomb had been exploded inside the float.

"You know," said Clarisse, "our float was a real crowd pleaser—until you misjudged those low-hanging oak branches on Beacon Street."

"People love to see parade floats get destroyed," Valentine said defensively. "The same as they like seeing Miss America trip on the runway."

"Well, they certainly cheered loudly enough . . ." She sipped her cola and then asked, "Did I miss anything while I was asleep?"

"You missed the Radical Lesbian Feminist Revolutionary Guerrilla Comedy Troupe. They did a very funny skit on Nancy Reagan and her gynecologist. You also missed— I'm happy to say—Mr. William Tunney's speech."

"Who?"

"The ex-communicated altar boy who's rabidly anti–organized religion. Last year he read a speech called 'Mutual Masturbation as a Revolutionary Act.' Remember?"

"Vaguely. And this year . . . ?" Clarisse prompted.

"This year, when he came up to the podium, he was wearing a black cassock and carrying a Bible. He read all the antihomosexual passages from Leviticus and St. Paul. After that, two friends brought on a flaming hibachi. Mr. Tunney ripped Leviticus and St. Paul out of the Bible and flung them into the flames. Then Mr. Tunney and his two friends applauded the smoke—no one else did, I'm happy to say."

Clarisse closed her eyes, shook her head, and then opened them again. The Captain swept past with the condom wobbling behind, valiantly trying to keep his footing on the slope. "Guess what we're going to see on the television news reports tonight," Clarisse said as she watched the departing couple. "Guess whose picture is going to be on the front page of the *Herald* tomorrow morning."

"Not those two you won't. The reading and viewing audiences of the greater Boston area are definitely not ready to look at a living, breathing prophylactic over their morning coffee. I've been watching them, and even the photographers from the gay papers are bending backwards not to get them in frame." Valentine glanced at his watch. "We promised Niobe we'd be back at the bar by five, and we have to get the keys to the truck back to Sean."

"Didn't he come to the parade?" asked Clarisse as she stood up.

71

"I called him while you were sleeping. He said he was still working on his tapes."

They made their way down the knoll through the mass of people, crossed Charles Street, and ambled into the Public Garden. On the bridge spanning the duck pond they leaned against the railing for a few moments. Small groups of people reclined on the grass about the perimeter of the pond and beneath the thriving willows and dying elms. Tourists milled in protective groups along the pathways among the vibrantly colored flower beds. The elegant swan boats glided lazily about the circumference of the pond. The noise from the rally on the nearby Common was surprisingly muted and vague.

They strolled on, out of the Garden and down the tree-lined mall bisecting Commonwealth Avenue, until they reached an apartment building at the corner of Exeter Street. They went up the stoop. Clarisse pressed the buzzer beneath the mailbox with Sean Alexander's name taped to it. They waited but got no reply. Valentine hit the button again, holding it for a long moment. Again they got no response.

"He's probably got the music cranked way up," Valentine said discontentedly. "And he said he had to have the key by six."

"Leave this one to me," said Clarisse, lighting nudging him aside.

She pushed the button at the end for a top-floor apartment. Receiving no reply, she immediately pressed the next button in line.

A scratchy voice came through the intercom speaker. "Yeah?"

"Sorry," Clarisse said into the speaker. "I pushed the wrong button. Sorry."

"Lovelace, what are you doing?"

Clarisse pressed a button for an apartment on the third floor. This time no voice came over the speaker, but the main door buzzed as the latch was released. Smiling triumphantly, Clarisse turned the knob and pushed open the door. "It never fails. There's always one tenant in every building

72

willing to buzz anybody in, sight unseen. It's why there are so many rapes, robberies, and murders in these places.''

They crossed the small foyer and went up the wide carpeted steps to the second landing. Sean's apartment was at the back of the building. As they approached his door, they glanced at one another. Quiet music was playing inside. They could even hear that Sean was whistling along with the melody. Valentine knocked on the door. They heard footsteps inside, but no one came to the door. Valentine knocked again and called out, ''Sean!'' Inside the apartment the telephone rang. Sean answered it, and they heard his voice and after a moment his laughter. Clarisse rapped her knuckles on the door. ''Sean?'' she called out.

Inside, Sean continued to talk on the telephone.

''I don't get it,'' Clarisse said to Valentine. ''I know he hears us.''

''Maybe he doesn't answer for anybody who doesn't call first.'' Valentine took the truck keys out of his pocket. ''What do I do about these?''

''Give them to me,'' said Sean, coming up the stairs of the building with a bag of groceries.

Clarisse and Valentine turned around quickly. She glanced at the apartment door and then back to Sean. Clarisse's features were streaked with questions.

''My guard dog,'' Sean offered with a grin.

Valentine was about to ask Sean to explain. Then he and Clarisse saw that Sean wasn't alone. A tall man wearing a Boston Gas Company uniform was coming up the stairs directly behind him. The man was broadly built, with severely short dark hair and a dark trimmed mustache. His uniform overalls were unzipped nearly to his navel, displaying thick hair curling on his chest.

''How you been, Daniel?'' said the gas man.

''Hello, Bander,'' Valentine answered coolly.

''Bander,'' Sean said, ''this is Clarisse.''

''Hello,'' Clarisse replied politely.

''I ran into Bander over at DeLuca's,'' Sean explained, pushing his apartment key into the lock and turning it.

73

"We dropped by to give you the Toyota keys," Valentine said. "It's parked on Charles by the Common."

Sean motioned for them to come inside. "How'd it go today?"

"We'll tell you all about it later," Valentine said hesitantly. "Niobe's holding down the fort alone. As soon as the rally starts to break up, half the South End'll head over to Slate. I hate to strand her."

"Oh, come on, Val. Just for a few minutes," Clarisse said. "Besides, I've never seen Sean's apartment."

Valentine said nothing, but his silence was clearly a reluctant acquiescence.

"My guard dog," Sean said again once all four of them were inside. The sound of his voice talking on the telephone was on tape, playing through two speakers.

He crossed the room and snapped off the taped conversation. He leaned to another tape machine and turned it on so that music filled the room.

"I record a typical evening at home. Whenever I leave the apartment, I play it back. Sounds just like somebody's in here. I can't afford a real security system, but this seems to work—I've never been broken into."

"Very clever," Clarisse said, genuinely impressed. She looked about the room.

Sean went down the connecting hallway and disappeared into the kitchen.

The apartment was a spacious one bedroom, with high ceilings and polished bare oak floors. The walls of the living room were nearly concealed by recording equipment—various sizes and makes of tape decks, amplifiers, and speakers. Several sets of headphones were lined up neatly on a counter, next to several piles of audiophile magazines. Wires and cords ran all around the room, at baseboard and at nearly ceiling level, as well. The only furniture was an overstuffed oatmeal-colored sofa and two comfortable-looking wingback chairs grouped about a massive glass coffee table. In one corner of the room was a large video receiver, three videocassette recorders, and four high stacks of cassette tapes on a small table beside it. In one of the barred windows overlooking the back alley hung a withered and dust-covered spider plant.

As soon as Sean was out of the room, the gas man made himself at home. Before he dropped into one of the wing-back armchairs, he turned the music up louder. "Anybody want to share a joint?" he asked, pulling one out of his pocket.

"No, thank you," Clarisse said amiably.

Valentine simply shook his head no without looking at the man. He was studying the titles on the videocassette tapes. After a moment he walked over and turned down the volume of the music.

"Long time no see, Daniel," said Bander, lighting the joint.

Valentine looked around at the man but remained silent. Clarisse watched both men with growing curiosity.

Sean came in, bringing with him a tray bearing four glasses of iced lemonade.

"Many thanks," said Clarisse, taking a glass before she seated herself on the couch. "It looks to me as if you could open your own recording studio right here in this apartment."

"That's exactly what I plan to do within the next year if I can swing it, but not here, of course."

Valentine, with a little groan, sank onto the end of the sofa opposite Clarisse. "Does this mean I'm going to have to search for another bartender?"

"No." Sean handed Valentine a glass of the lemonade. "I like working at Slate. I wouldn't want to give that up. Not unless Warner Records comes after me with a multi-million-dollar contract for my services."

Clarisse watched the gas-company repairman as Valentine and Sean talked. The man seemed at ease, though he didn't make the least effort to join in the conversation. He drank off the lemonade in one long swallow and returned to his joint. He kept time to the music with one bobbing foot thrown over the arm of the chair. Bander turned suddenly and caught Clarisse off guard, evaluating him. "Is this talent show your bar's sponsoring tonight going to be another tired drag show or what?'' he asked. "I hate tacky queens who get done up in gold lamé and cheap wigs and lip-sync 'I Am What I Am' for the two hundred zillionth time. It makes me want to—how do you say?—puke.''

"Then don't come,'' snapped Valentine.

"Last time I went to a talent show,'' Bander went on, "it was emceed by this big fat drag queen wearing earrings made out of VISA credit cards and a red-glittered toilet seat for a necklace. You getting something like that to emcee your show? Some fat tacky drag queen who wears earrings made out of credit cards?''

"I am emceeing the show tonight,'' Clarisse replied coldly, "and I will not be wearing credit cards or a toilet seat.''

Bander shrugged, unperturbed. He looked at Valentine. "You think you'll draw a crowd tonight? Lots of talk about your bar around town. Lots of people not going there anymore.''

"What talk?'' Sean asked.

"You know. People saying you ought to rename the place 'The Terminal Bar.' Have a new advertising slogan— 'Drop In/Drop Dead.' Start selling T-shirts with 'I Tricked out of Slate and Lived' printed on 'em.''

"Our business,'' Clarisse said tightly, "is fine.''

Bander grinned, one eyebrow arched. "So gay men like to live dangerously. So what's new?''

"Anybody for more lemonade?'' Sean offered suddenly.

"No,'' Valentine said. "We have to leave.''

"My condolences to your customers,'' Bander said.

Sean walked Valentine and Clarisse to the door and stepped out into the hall with them. "I don't know what all that was about in there, but I'm sorry. But, well, I like Bander.''

"It's all right, Sean,'' Valentine said. "Bander and I go back a few years—that's all. Thanks for the lemonade.''

"See you at eight,'' Clarisse added with a parting smile.

Once on Commonwealth Avenue again, Clarisse asked Valentine, "What's the story?''

"Bander and I go back a long way,'' Valentine repeated

ruefully. "In fact, Bander goes back a long way with most of the gay men in Boston."

"Does he really work for Boston Gas, or was that uniform just a costume?"

"You know that old fantasy about making it with the man who comes to repair something?" Valentine said. "Well, for several thousand men in Boston, Bander has made that a fantasy come true."

"Is that how you met him?"

Valentine nodded.

"So why are you on such bad terms now—other than the fact that he's one's of the most unpleasant people on the East Coast?"

"A few years ago Bander went home with a friend of mine named Gary. Gary was into mild bondage and discipline."

"Mild bondage?" Clarisse asked skeptically. "Is that like getting tied up with rubber bands?"

"Just about. He liked to be tied up, but he always made sure he could get out of it in two seconds flat. He also liked to get slapped around, but no marks. It was just fantasy for him. Anyway, he went home with Bander once. They did some sort of drugs, and Gary ended up tied to the kitchen table with a black eye, a broken front tooth, and two cracked ribs. His landlady found him like that the next day."

"What did Gary do? Did he press charges?"

"No. But one night he did confront Bander in the Ramrod. Bander just said, 'Hey, man, that's what you said you were into. And when you kept saying, "No, no, stop," I figured that was just part of the scene.' "

"That's a pretty rotten attitude," Clarisse said quietly.

"That's Bander all over," Valentine said.

They turned up Berkeley Street in the direction of the South End and walked on in silence.

chapter
nine

ALTHOUGH VARIOUS POLITICAL ORGANIZATIONS WERE
sponsoring events on the evening of Gay Pride Day, it was
the talent show mounted by Slate that attracted the largest
crowd of the evening. The $350 prize for the night's best
act, to be determined by audience applause, had proved to
be a wise crowd-drawing strategy on Valentine's part.

In the back area of the bar a small dais had been constructed before a red velvet curtain across the back wall.
Behind this were concealed doors to the small kitchen and
the ladies' room, both areas being used as changing rooms
for the various performers. Sean had persuaded two friends
who were theatrical lighting technicians to donate their tal-
ents and equipment for the evening. A small portable stereo
unit was set up to one side of the staging to accommodate
those performers who'd brought their own music on records and cassette tapes. A woman friend of Niobe's, who
went by the name Regular Ethel, was stationed by the machine to make sure the right recordings were played at the
right times. She was a sharp-featured young woman who
wore a red sequined strapless minidress, black hose, and

black heels. Her black hair formed a helmet about her head. She chewed gum and cracked it to irritating effect.

By a quarter to ten Slate was filled to capacity. A number of performers in the show, some of them already in costume, mingled with their friends or leaned against the bar, conspicuously downing complimentary drinks. Rock music filled the barroom. Overhead the fans whirled, lazily stirring the artificially cooled, smoky air. Niobe had left at six o'clock in such haste that she had forgotten to take her pet canary. Someone had tied Rodan's cage to one of the blades. Squawking continuously and littering the air with tiny tufts of yellow feather, the bird was still going around and around in slow, dizzying circles.

At five minutes to the hour, Clarisse swept down the connecting spiral stairs into the empty coat-check room. She edged her way up to the bar as Valentine was returning with change for a customer. He stopped short, spilled the coins into the customer's outstretched hand, and exclaimed, "Tell me that's not a permanent."

A puff of curls framed Clarisse's forehead, held in place by a white-on-maroon polka-dot silk scarf tied up into a bow atop her head. Her bolero-sleeved blouse was of cream-colored rayon. She wore a pair of maroon satin toreador pants and gold lamé sling-back sandals. Gold hoops dangling from her earlobes completed the outfit.

Clarisse leaned sideways to check her image in the bar mirror. "It's my Lucille Ball Cold War look. Like it?"

'You want a drink before you assume your stage duties?" Valentine replied, not quite answering her question. "If you don't need one, I think I do."

Clarisse looked at the clock. "Send one over to the stage. I have to get things rolling in a few minutes."

A tall wan man wearing a blond bubble-cut wig and a pink organdy prom gown with spaghetti straps thrust himself up to the bar next to Clarisse and addressed Valentine. "Is this the place where they're holding the cotillion? I've been to Chaps, Buddies, and Fritz, but nobody knows where the cotillion's being held. I know there's a cotillion going on somewhere!"

"We're having a talent show here," Clarisse offered.

"Jacques," Valentine explained. "Over in Bay Village. They're having a cotillion tonight."

Clarisse started to say something, but the man exploded into a flurry of movement, pummeling customers right and left as he flounced out toward the street.

Clarisse looked at Valentine with a tight smile. "Jacques is not having a cotillion tonight, as you very well know. Jacques is featuring Competition Transsexual Mud Wrestling. Not many contestants, but the ones they have are really into it."

Valentine shrugged. "Same thing in my book." Valentine pointed to the bar clock. "Show time. Break your neck."

"That's *leg*."

Clarisse made her way to the back of the bar. Regular Ethel handed her a wireless microphone and turned on the stereo as Clarisse stepped up to the edge of the stage. Clarisse nodded to Sean, and he snapped off the house music just as Regular Ethel dropped the stereo arm onto a record.

Clarisse quickly straightened her blouse and flashed a bright smile. The bar's lights were lowered, and a spotlight winked on, wavered a few moments, and then snagged on center stage. Clarisse strode across the dais, hitting the spot just as a recording of "Rabid Killer Mama" blasted from the overhead speakers wired into Regular Ethel's stereo.

Clarisse turned on the woman with a glare. "Ethel," she shouted above the music, "that is not my theme music!"

Ethel swiped the needle off the record. "Sorry, sorry, sorry," she called out, and frantically flipped through the stack of albums beside her stool, madly snapping her chewing gum.

"Never mind now," Clarisse told her with a patient sigh, and turned to the audience. "Obviously," she said, her voice suddenly amplified by the microphone that had just been turned on, "that was not 'There's No Business Like Show Business.' "

"It was the Slug Dogs," came Ethel's voice, tinny and distant and unamplified.

"Thank you, Ethel."

"Anytime, anytime."

"I'm Clarisse Lovelace, and this is Gay Pride Day—and you're all in Slate, I presume, because you're all expecting to be knocked right down to the floor with the talent that's going to be presented up here tonight for your consideration, your edification, and your incredible enjoyment. It's a lineup you haven't seen before—I can guarantee you that. You're going to see talent you didn't even know existed. People dug in the backs of the backs of their closets for *these* costumes, let me tell you. People took mail-order correspondence courses, people saw the Streisand *A Star is Born* fifteen times just to get the gestures right, people made last-minute visits to their chiropractors, people have gone to just an astounding amount of trouble to make you happy tonight. So I am expecting audience response—has everybody got that? And got it good? I want the needle on the Applause-O-Meter to go right off the scale!"

The audience applauded riotously.

Clarisse smiled. "Then let's get this show on the road! Our first act is Joey Manzarello and Fifi Mandelbaum! Let's give Joey and Fifi a big hand."

Applause rose and then petered out when Clarisse melted away and Joey and Fifi came on. Joey was a skinny, peroxided young man who brought a twelve-string guitar and a stool with him. He dropped the stool center stage and wriggled up onto it. Fifi was a small and dark woman with curly black hair and wore a loose coral smock over a pair of tight designer jeans. She carried another stool out with her. Arranging it slightly behind her partner's, she sat down and gave Regular Ethel the cue. Regular Ethel dropped the needle down on a record. Neil Sedaka's voice spilled out of the speakers, singing about unrequited love. Joey pretended to be playing the guitar as he lip-synced the words of the ballad. Just behind him, Fifi interpreted the lyrics in sign language as she swayed dreamily to the rhythm of the music.

The audience was silent—out of astonishment, Clarisse suspected, more than out of admiration.

The applause at the end was polite but uncertain.

The second act was a tall, thin man who would give his name only as "Dallas Ralph." Dallas Ralph was dressed as Dale Evans. He tap-danced and jumped rope at the same time to a lively recording of "The Yellow Rose of Texas." From the back of the bar a drunken man shouted, "My God, it's a dancing asshole!" but the rest of the audience was more appreciative. Dallas Ralph received generous applause when he finished, and the only boos were from Joey Manzarello and Fifi Mandelbaum, who were now upset that they had had to go on first.

The remainder of the first half of the talent show consisted of a man in a doctor's uniform reading aloud from the Fleet Company's essay "A History of the Enema"; an inebriated drag queen who passed out facedown on the stage halfway through a lip sync of "There Is Nothing Like a Dame"; two women, dressed as men, dramatizing a scene from John Irving's *Hotel New Hampshire*; a frail young woman with black hair who sang a medley of Janis Joplin tunes as if they'd been written by Joni Mitchell; a stand-up comic who conducted an "on the street" interview with a plaster chicken; a man dressed in a sari and carrying a bottle of Heinz catsup who reenacted the assassination of Indira Gandhi, with Regular Ethel playing recorded machine-gun fire; three men, disguised as the Gabor sisters, singing "Boogie-Woogie Bugle Boy" with Hungarian accents; a female singer who did a throaty imitation of Billie Holiday; and a man costumed as Queen Elizabeth II who yodeled "God Save the Queen" and then sang the words in French.

Clarisse announced the final act of the first half: "A new country-and-western band from Springfield called Patty LaParty and the Joy Boys." The audience clapped in expectation but was obviously disappointed when a single guitar player shambled out on stage, plugged his instrument into the amplifier, and began tuning. But after a few moments a mustached man wearing a Loretta Lynn wig, a denim skirt, and a sequined blouse trounced up on stage, saying, "Hi, I'm Patty LaParty, and this is my Joy Boy. My first song goes out tonight to my ex-husband, Hank, and if he's in the audience—and probably he is—then it's all for him." Patty LaParty had not gotten five bars into the song when the *real* Patty LaParty lurched up on stage— this Patty was a genuine female. She tore off the man's wig and skirt, grabbed the microphone, and said, "Hi, I'm Patty LaParty, and these are the Joy Boys. My first song goes out tonight to my ex-husband, Hank, and if he's in the audience—and probably he is—then it's all for him." At which point, the ex-husband, Hank—in chaps and cowboy hat and lasso—swung up on stage and joined his ex-wife. They sang of "A Book in a Plain Brown Wrapper" that had broken up their marriage.

The audience demanded a second song. Patty LaParty, the Joy Boys, and Hank did a four-part *a cappella* rendition of "O Holy Night" while their bass guitar showered them with handfuls of glitter like snow. When the quartet reached the chorus, "Fall on your knees," they actually fell to their knees, on small sequined pillows they had held concealed behind them.

At the bar, Valentine and Sean had stopped serving drinks—simply because everyone in the room had crowded forward to watch Patty LaParty and the Joy Boys. It was a few minutes in which to clear away the accumulated glasses and bottles.

A banging noise came loud and demanding to Valentine's left. He looked down toward the front of the room and saw Bander in his Boston Gas overalls at the end of the bar near the entrance. He was staring directly at Valentine. He let go of an empty beer bottle, and it rattled on the mahogany surface of the bar.

Valentine nudged Sean and arched his head in Bander's direction. "The gas bag is here to see you."

Sean looked down at the bar, then back to the stage. "No, he's not," Sean said pointedly. "We had an argument this afternoon right after you and Clarisse left my place. You're right; he's a jerk."

Sean moved away to wait on a customer who was signaling to him. Valentine went down to the opposite end of the bar.

"Sean doesn't want to talk to you," Valentine told Bander.

"I don't want to talk to him, either. I'm here on official business." He flicked a finger against the Boston Gas logo sewn on his overalls.

"What are you talking about?"

"Somebody here called repair. Said there was the smell of gas in an apartment upstairs. Second floor. I'm here to check it out."

Valentine looked doubtful. "Who called? I didn't, and neither did Sean, and Clarisse didn't say anything."

"I don't know who it was," Bander said. "If you don't believe me, call repair yourself and check it out."

Valentine glanced behind him toward the stage. He could see no more of Clarisse than the top of her polka-dot scarf. "Maybe it was Clarisse," he speculated, "and she forgot to tell me with all the excitement tonight."

"So, what'll it be—I check it, or you risk blowing this place straight to hell?"

At that moment applause erupted for the country-and-western group and the end of the first half of the show. Still clapping, the audience swerved around toward the bar, half of them already reaching out with bills clutched in their hands.

"Oh, Jesus," Valentine said with a sigh, "here they come."

"I need your keys," Bander insisted.

Valentine yanked them from a back pocket and tossed them to the repairman. "Outside and up through the stairwell entrance," he ordered as he rushed down the bar to meet the oncoming tide.

"What did he want?" Sean asked as he flicked on the tape machine. But the sudden music was so loud and the demands of the customers were so frantic that Valentine didn't have a chance to reply. A few minutes later, when Clarisse finally worked her way up to the bar, asking for a

84

bottle of Chivas Regal and a straw, the incident had gone right out of Valentine's head.

CLARISSE SPENT THE BREAK IN CONSULTATION WITH REGular Ethel, making certain that all the music was correctly marked and put in the needed order. The second half of the show was to be shorter in case the crowd was growing inattentive. After she was satisfied that Regular Ethel had a grip on the situation, Clarisse edged into the ladies' room to talk to the second-act performers who were struggling into costume and makeup. As soon as she had prepared everyone, she hurried back to the bar and downed another scotch. As she was trying to make up her mind whether or not to have another, the lights lowered.

Clarisse threaded her way back to the stage. She had one foot already on the dais and was about to step up on it when someone in the crowd jostled her and she fell backward. But not to the floor—hands caught her.

"Thank you," she was about to say, but didn't. For the hands that had caught her did not let go, nor did they help then to raise her to the stage. The hands—and there were a number of them—were exploratory.

She looked about sharply.

It was a woman who had caught her around the waist. B.J.—the initials flashed in Clarisse's mind. The two men were there, too. Ruder and Cruder, on either side, and they had her arms.

"Nice," B.J. said, massaging Clarisse's back, "like a strong, young boy."

"Good muscle tone," Cruder said as he rubbed two fingers smoothly along the inside of her elbow.

"Yeah," Ruder agreed as he prodded underneath her arm.

"Would you like to see my teeth?" demanded Clarisse, pulling away from all three at once. "They're good, too."

Ruder looked at her, and one of the amber stage lights flashed in the lenses of his silvered dark glasses. "This better be a good show,'' he said in a surprisingly resonant voice.

"Yeah,'' Cruder added, "this better be a barrel of fucking laughs.''

Clarisse turned from them sharply and climbed up on stage. She turned around with a broad smile. "I know you're all—''

Regular Ethel slammed a finger onto the tape play button of the tape deck. Kate Smith singing "God Bless America'' filled the barroom.

"Not yet!'' Clarisse screamed.

Kate Smith shut up.

"Oh, God,'' cried Regular Ethel, "you are confusing me totally!''

Clarisse closed her eyes for a moment and smiled a temporizing smile. It didn't help that B.J. and her two boyfriends in black leather were standing right at the foot of the stage, staring up at her and whispering. Clarisse looked over their heads.

"Let's give a hand to Regular Ethel, who's trying very hard!''

There was applause, and during that applause Clarisse recovered herself.

"Now, for the first act of this second half of the show, I would like everyone to give a great big hand to—''

The curtain at the back of the stage opened dramatically, and in the darkness there was a glimmering suggestion of a figure.

"Now Ethel,'' hissed Clarisse.

Kate Smith came back on in the third bar of "God Bless America.''

"—Mr. Twirlin' Whirlin'!''

Clarisse leaped down from the stage, for she knew what was coming. Mr. Twirlin' Whirlin'—a short, fat Hispanic man about forty—surged out between the red curtains on roller skates. He was twirling a baton dramatically above his head, changing hands and spinning his entire body about as he glided along the rim of the stage. Mr. Twirlin' Whirlin' wore a headband with two small American flags attached to the end of springs, a silver sleeveless shirt encrusted with white-and-blue blinking lights, and skin-tight red-and-white satin shorts. His roller skates were red and white; his athletic socks, blue. He flung his baton into the air with one hand and caught it with the other and then performed the same feat while bent far forward and reaching up between his legs behind himself.

When Kate Smith was done, so was Mr. Twirlin's Whirlin', but the audience demanded an encore. Mr. Whirlin' was evidently prepared for this, for after a few seconds of blank tape, Kate Smith went into the "Ballad of the Green Berets." Regular Ethel hit the light switch, and the stage was in darkness—except for the nubs of Mr. Twirlin' batons, which glowed a phosphorescent yellow.

The people in Slate who had remained for the second act were glad that they did, for even though there were only four performances, each was, in its way, very special. After Mr. Whirlin' came a large woman dressed in a muu muu that had been silk-screened with silhouette images of Lassie. Her name was Rona Barrette, and she wore a half-dozen barrettes on her lank brown hair. She was accompanied by a collie named Clover, and Clover wore barrettes, too. Clover was a well-behaved dog and sat when he was told to sit. Rona Barrette announced, "Clover is the smartest dog in the world. Clover can talk." Rona Barrette knelt down on the stage next to Clover, placed her pudgy hands around Clover's muzzle, and squeezed. "Talk," Rona Barrette said to the collie. Then, to the intense astonishment of the crowd, Clover said, "Hamburger."

"More! More!" screamed the audience, but Rona Barrette said, "Not unless I win this contest. If Clover and me win this contest, then I'll come back out, and Clover will talk some more. But only if we win. Got that, you people?"

"More! More!" the crowd shouted, but Rona Barrette and Clover returned to the ladies' room to wait out the end of the show.

The third act was a bartender from Rhode Island who did the shimmy while dressed as Our Lady of Fatima.

"And now," said Clarisse weakly when both she and the audience had recovered from the bartender's display, "we have the final act of the evening. It's the one I know you've all been waiting for. This is a young woman we all know from *Boston Magazine* and the 'Channel Five Evening Report'—a young woman who has been arrested more times than any other street performer in Boston. You've seen her jeered at on the Common, you've seen her jostled out of the way in front of Filene's, you've heard her being drowned out by the subways at Park Street Under, you've watched her dry her rain-soaked clothing on the fence outside this very establishment. This evening, she tells me, is the first time that she has worked indoors in two years, so I want you all to give a warm welcome to—"

The audience was already clapping, because they knew who it was.

"—Miss Ruby Charisma! In her brand-new act, never seen before, of the Moth and the Candle Flame!"

Felix and George, the Slate runners, came out of the ladies' room, bearing with them what looked to be a large cocoon. It was in reality a sheet with the hems basted together. The cocoon was left alone on stage in the spotlight. It began to writhe obscenely, as if in a Disney nature film. It split open at the top, and after some struggle, a young woman emerged. She had a round, vacuous face and kinky black hair. Kicking the torn cocoon aside, she looked around as if she were seeing the world for the first time.

She was wearing a black leotard and cape, and when she tentatively raised her arms, she revealed wings with great spots of luminous violet and red. She began to flutter around the stage, like the moth she was costumed to be.

Felix came back onto the stage, bearing a lighted candle.

Ruby Charisma was fascinated by the candle. She danced around it, humming her own accompaniment through clenched teeth. She went ever closer to the flame until she had lit the small sponge that was hung around her neck on a string. It had evidently been soaked in cold fire and burned brightly on her breast. Then Ruby went into a slow death agony, humming Chopin's funeral march, her moth life and the lurid flame on her breast expiring at the same moment.

Rona Barrette and the promise of more speech from Clover were completely forgotten.

The Applause-O-Meter went right off the scale for Ruby Charisma.

chapter
ten

"WHAT HAPPENED?" ASKED CLARISSE, LOOKING AROUND with apparent surprise. It was only twenty minutes after Ruby Charisma had received her $350 prize for the talent show. The crowd that had viewed and cheered and laughed with all the acts was almost gone. The twenty or so patrons who remained in Slate were scattered listlessly against the walls or sat nursing beers at the bar. "Where did everybody go all of a sudden? Did Saturday night suddenly shut down?"

"Self-preservation took over," Valentine said with a grimace. He stood behind the bar, transferring bottles of beer into a cooler. "As soon as the show was over, everybody decided that Slate wasn't the safest place in the world to be, so they went somewhere safer, and more exciting."

"Safe?" Clarisse said with a scowl. "This bar isn't safe? There are five police cruisers parked practically at the front door. District D is less than a hundred feet away—"

"I'm talking about murders, Lovelace, not muggings. It's gotten around that the necktie killer hangs out here in Slate. Bander wasn't just being flip this afternoon when he said people were staying away from here. People are worried enough about picking up AIDS. You think they're also going to risk ending up like Jed and the All-American Boy and—''

"So we spent over a thousand dollars to set up this evening, and everybody leaves five minutes after the show's over. Boy, that's ingratitude," Clarisse said loftily.

"Not everybody's gone," said Valentine. "The cops are still here."

Clarisse swiveled slowly around on the stool. "There are cops in here?" She glanced over the tiny crowd.

"Since Jed was killed, they've been stopping by here almost every night before closing time. This evening they've been in here since the show began.''

Clarisse turned back around and put down her glass. "Why haven't you told me this before now?" she asked soberly. "Why were you holding back?"

"Because I didn't want you worrying about it, and I didn't want you thinking every other man who came in here was a cop.''

"What does this say about the trust that exists between you and me?" Clarisse exclaimed. "Did you tell Sean? I'll bet you did. Did you tell Niobe?"

Two men sitting a few stools down at the bar glanced over at Valentine and Clarisse as if waiting to hear more of the argument.

Valentine made a sharp motion for her to lower her voice. "Don't get hysterical." He tossed the empty box and leaned his elbows on the bar as he spoke in a low, confidential tone.

"Niobe doesn't know about it, and neither does Sean, but I suppose it really wouldn't be fair not to let you in on it. When the cops talked to me after Jed was killed, they told me they were putting this place under surveillance. They told me not to tell anybody else, and I said, 'Does that include Clarisse, my best friend in the world?' and they said yes, it did. And that's why I didn't tell you.''

Clarisse smiled. "All right, I get the picture." She looked past him to the mirror behind the bar. "Where are the cops? Point them out to me. I hate being watched without knowing who's doing the watching."

"I promised I wouldn't." Valentine hedged.

Clarisse's mouth dropped. "I cannot believe you're saying this to me. Me, who would walk over white-hot coals and eat raw anchovies if it would help you."

Valentine relented but said seriously, "Promise you'll keep a very tight lid on this. It really is important, Lovelace."

"I swear on the very earth that will cover me one day. Where are they?"

"Keep looking in the mirror. Now, you see the guy leaning against the cigarette machine? The one with the mustache, wearing the tank top?"

"That hunk?"

"And the guy against the mirror with the five o'clock shadow beard wearing the green T-shirt and denim cutoffs?"

"The blond bombshell?"

"Now, look over there. See B.J. and her two friends? Follow their heavy cruise to the one with no shirt and the leather vest."

"The clone with the mustache?" Clarisse drew her eyes away from the glass and eyed Valentine suspiciously. "Did you handpick them?"

"Clarisse, the cops know better than to try to smoke out a killer with a troll or somebody who looks like an obvious misfit. And for God's sake, if they come in while you're on, don't offer them free drinks."

Clarisse studied the three policemen in the mirror once more. "You don't suppose they put gay cops on this detail, do you? Those three look too right, too comfortable."

"Not when you watch closely. They can't quite pull it off. They've got the hair okay, and they've got the clothes down, but they can't get the eyes right. They don't know how to cruise, and they're probably looking for a man walking around with ties trailing out of his back pocket."

Clarisse heaved a sigh and slid her glass across to Valentine. "More scotch, please. I'm depressed. It's Saturday night. It's Gay Pride Weekend, and fifty percent of our clientele thinks the other fifty percent are murder suspects. Two months ago this was the hottest bar in town, and now look around. This place is about as popular as the lower deck lounge of the *Titanic*."

"I called your uncle this week—" said Valentine.

"You called Noah? You didn't tell me that, either!"

"I told him business is falling off because of this."

"What did he say?"

"He gave me a bit of advice."

"Which was?"

"Find the murderer."

Clarisse clicked her tongue. "Easy for him to say from the safe distance of Morocco."

Valentine looked around the bar. Three men walked out together. No one came in to bring the population back up again. "I wish *I* were in Morocco," he said with a sigh.

"I wish we were both in Morocco now," Clarisse said. "Better yet, I think you ought to stay here and worry and fret and let me go off for a relaxing week or so in an exotic foreign country."

The house lights came on at two A.M., and at two-fifteen the last of the customers wandered out. The three plain-clothesmen lingered on the sidewalk beneath the street lamp, but no offers were made to them, and eventually—with surreptitious nods to one another—they wandered off.

Sean snatched up empty bottles and glasses from around the room while Valentine cashed out the register. Clarisse had already gone up to bed. Felix and George, the two bar runners, began the preliminary clean-up, a job they'd finish in the morning at ten.

At three A.M., Valentine closed the door on Sean, Felix, and George and snapped off the barroom lights. In the darkness, he climbed the spiral stairs to his office.

At his desk, he opened a small stack of bills and mail that he hadn't had time to tend to that day. He pulled out the checkbook and started to write out checks but found he lacked concentration for even this simple task. He opened and read a long letter he'd received from a friend in San

Francisco but lost interest in that, as well. For a long moment Valentine sat in his desk chair, facing the two-way glass. He stared blankly into the darkened barroom below, glanced at the clock, and then pushed himself out of the chair. With a noisy yawn, he snapped out the light and left the office, yawning once again as he went up the stairs to the floor above. He unlocked the door to his apartment and went inside.

Valentine hesitated before flipping the lock of the apartment door. A light from his bedroom made a rectangle across the living-room carpet. He tried to remember if he'd turned off all the lights in the place before he went downstairs to work for the evening. He stood very still and listened. His brow creased in question as he became aware of soft music from inside the bedroom—jazz, just the sort of music he liked least. Valentine knew he had not left the radio playing, and certainly not to that station. Cautiously, he stepped up to the door and peered through the crack.

Valentine froze when he saw the silhouetted shadow of a human form rise up against the bedroom wall.

"What took so long?" a masculine voice inquired casually.

The shadow receded across the wall as Valentine went into the bedroom. Bander was completing a lazy stretch and settling back into the pillows propped against the headboard of the bed. He wore only a pair of low-rise navy-blue briefs. His tanned body was dark against the rust-and-cream striped sheets. His Boston Gas overalls were draped over the ladder-back chair before one of the front windows, shoes underneath the chair. On the nightstand a lighted cigarette rested within easy reach on the lip of a saucer. The shade of the lamp on the stand had been tilted away from the bed, diffusing the already low light and casting Bander in evocative shadow. He looked as if he'd taken some care to arrange himself to maximal erotic effect, legs slightly parted, one arm up behind his head.

He picked the cigarette out of the saucer and took a drag on it. "I asked what took you so long," Bander repeated. Smoke spiraled up from his mouth.

"What the hell are you doing here?" Valentine demanded as he came into the room. Although he did not raise his voice, his anger was clear.

Bander tapped ash into the saucer. "Couldn't find an ashtray anywhere. I thought you were a smoker."

"I asked you a question," Valentine said coldly.

Bander rubbed a hand across his chest, fingers deliberately caressing the curve of one pectoral before grazing down his muscle-plated stomach and coming to rest on his crotch. He sat up slightly and stabbed out his cigarette in the center of the saucer. "You gave me your keys, remember?" He nodded toward the oak bureau next to the door, then fell back against the pillows. "Somebody told me your bedroom had a perfect view into the locker room of the police station across the street. I watched for a long time, but there wasn't anything worth seeing. When's the change in shift?"

"I don't give a damn about the view. I know *how* you got up here. I want to know *why* you're here!"

"I fixed your pilot light," replied Bander easily. "It had gone out."

"You didn't get any repair call to come here, did you?"

Bander only grinned.

"What's to keep me from calling up Boston Gas and reporting you?"

Unruffled, Bander shrugged. "I wrote up a report call before I left. When I got up here, I called to verify I was working. On the books, I went off duty at two A.M. If there's some problem, I'll just say you invited me to stay."

Shaking his head, Valentine folded his arms and leaned against the bureau. "You used to have the morals of a rabid dog. I see they've degenerated."

"Well, I *am* here, so why don't we just deal with that?" His voice was warm now, friendly. "Listen, I know what bartenders are like at three A.M. The customers have cut out, but their adrenaline's up, and they're ready to play."

"I'm not."

Bander ignored this. His hand was still on the crotch of

his dark blue underpants. "When I saw you over at Sean's this afternoon, I started thinking how hot you used to be."

"Really? Is that why you were so damned pleasant over there?"

"You were with what's-her-name," Bander said dismissively.

"Her name is Clarisse," Valentine said shortly.

Bander raised his eyes. They were dilated and moist. "Hey, I didn't lay myself out here to talk about some woman."

Valentine took Bander's uniform off the back of the chair and shook the wrinkles out of it. He then folded it twice over his arm, stepped across the room, and flung it out the open window.

Bander shot up in bed. "What are you doing?"

"Sorry," Valentine said. "My hand slipped." He grabbed Bander's work boots from beneath the chair and tossed them out the window, as well. Valentine smiled as he heard the boots hit the sidewalk two floors below.

"You jerk!" Bander spat as he sprang from the bed. "I don't believe this!" He gripped the sill and thrust himself halfway out the window. "I don't *believe* you—" He stopped and barked loudly, "Get away from those things!"

Valentine stepped over to the other window and leaned out. On the sidewalk below, one of the derelicts from the playground was eagerly gathering up the discarded overalls and shoes.

Bander's face reddened. Veins strained in his neck. "Goddamn you!" he shouted.

The derelict scurried back across the sidewalk and into the dark safety of the playground.

Bander and Valentine pulled back inside the apartment. Bander's fists clasped and unclasped with rage, his mouth was set tightly, his eyes were glazed with anger. He thrust himself forward, his hands clawing for Valentine's neck.

The man's rage made him clumsy. Valentine easily seized Bander's right arm and flipped him about. Saliva sprayed from between Bander's clenched teeth, and he yelped as his captured arm was jerked painfully upward.

Valentine shoved him stumbling out of the bedroom and across the darkened living room. He deftly got the apartment door unlocked and flung it wide. He slapped one palm against the wall switch, and pools of light illuminated the stairs all the way down to the street entrance. Valentine, his free hand on the railing, got the two of them down the steps without falling. He unlatched and raked wide the street door in one forceful motion. Valentine released Bander's arm and pushed the nearly naked man out across the sidewalk.

"Run and you can make it home before dawn," Valentine offered. "Anyone sees you, they'll just think you're an exhibitionistic jogger."

"You lousy scum," Bander growled, "I'll fuckin' make you pay for this."

Valentine slammed shut the street door.

Back in his apartment, Valentine got undressed and took a quick shower before climbing into bed. As he reached to snap out the nightstand light, he noticed that his closet was ajar. Hanging from the inside doorknob were at least a half-dozen neckties. Valentine sat up and stared at the ties. He rarely wore them. He'd given to charity all but a half dozen. Those were always kept neatly folded on one side of his top bureau drawer—not on the doorknob of the closet.

chapter eleven

"MY GOD," VALENTINE SAID WITH MOCK ASTONISHMENT, "I was expecting Medusa's daughter, and I get Little Mary Sunshine."

Clarisse, carrying her telephone with her as she answered her apartment door and with the receiver tucked securely between her left ear and shoulder, motioned him to silence.

It was eight forty-five on Sunday morning, and Valentine had shown up at her threshold with a pot of freshly brewed coffee and a string-tied box of muffins.

Clarisse took the round glass pot from him. Valentine kicked the door shut behind them and followed her across the room to a table by an open back window. He placed the box next to the electric warmer on which Clarisse placed the pot. The table was already set for two, complete with a slender vase of fresh-cut orange-and-yellow tiger lilies. Valentine gave her a puzzled look, which she ignored, and then sat down.

"Fascinating," Clarisse muttered into the receiver. "I

never knew . . ." She covered the mouthpiece briefly enough to whisper, "Be off in a second, Val."

Silently, Valentine mouthed the question Who is it?

Clarisse again briefly covered the mouthpiece. "Paul Harvey," she replied. "Would you like your buns warmed?"

"*The* Paul Harvey?" Valentine said aloud. "The news commentator Paul Harvey?"

"Shh!" Clarisse snapped, and then added a nod to his question. "Amazing," she said into the receiver.

Valentine watched her with growing curiosity. Clarisse opened the refrigerator and retrieved a tub of soft butter from a lower shelf. She transferred a generous amount to a small plate and carried it to the table. She seated herself opposite Valentine and undid the string about the box of pastries and tossed it into the trash can between the stove and the refrigerator. "*Un*believable," she said with a soft click of her tongue as she rested her elbows on the table. A balmy morning breeze gently rustled the long, curved petals of the tiger lilies and pushed at Clarisse's hair. As she listened, she gazed out the window at Tremont Street a block away. Her Lucille Ball puff of the previous night was gone and her hair repaged. She wore a loose-fitting melon-colored blouse, jeans, and sandals. The palest hint of rose rouge tinted her cheeks. She turned suddenly away from the window.

"Fine," she said briskly. "Good day to you, too, Paul."

Clarisse hung up and flipped open the box of muffins.

"Why in the world would Paul Harvey call *you*?" Valentine asked suspiciously.

"He was telling me everything there was to know about German cockroaches," she confided. She tilted the box in Valentine's direction. "Which would you like? Orange, cranberry, walnut, or blueberry?"

Valentine selected the blueberry and put it on his plate. Clarisse filled their mugs with coffee. "I never knew cockroaches—*German* cockroaches," she amended, "could be so interesting. They're a growing problem in this country,

99

you know. Paul tells me they could become a plague if something isn't done about them.''

Valentine put his knife and muffin down. He looked about the kitchen with widened eyes. ''Have I just stumbled into the Twilight Zone?''

Clarisse edged the telephone over in front of him. ''Answer it,'' she directed.

''It didn't ring. Are you on drugs? Is that why you look so fresh this morning?''

''Just answer it.''

Reluctantly, Valentine lifted the receiver and put it to his ear. He listened a moment and then covered the mouthpiece with his palm and said to Clarisse, ''It's Sister Rozinnia. She says the Virgin Mary is going to appear next Friday evening at the Medford Twin Drive-In with an important message for mankind.''

''That's certainly going to make it an interesting evening for all those teenagers showing up to see *Roller Zombies* and *Sorority Girls in the House of Pain*.'' Clarisse turned the point of her knife toward him. ''You don't have to cover the receiver. No one can hear you.''

''What's going on, anyway?'' he asked, hanging up the telephone.

''I've been getting radio stations on that thing for nearly an hour. I was about to call you when I got Paul Harvey instead, talking about roaches.'' She shrugged. ''I wouldn't mind so much if it were FM at least . . .''

Valentine pulled his muffin apart and generously spread one side with butter. ''You know, I thought I'd find you still in your bathrobe, nerves and hair frazzled, stumbling bleary-eyed from wall to wall. Instead, you look as bright as these tiger lilies.''

''Which, by the way, I bought this morning at the Greek market down the street.''

Valentine furrowed his brow. ''Are you sure you're not sick or on something?''

''What I am, Mr. Valentine, is a professional woman.''

''Oh, yeah?''

''Yeah. I've decided that if I'm going to be a viable

partner in the running of this bar, I'm going to do it right. Positions of responsibility suit me quite well—I think.''

''You'll do fine,'' he said, idly snatching unsuccessfully at a large fly that had just flown through the window, headed for the muffins.

''Thank you for that incredible vote of confidence. A true friend—whether he felt it or not—might have forced a *little* enthusiasm.''

''I'm not feeling too enthusiastic just now. Sorry.''

''Bad night?''

''Moderately awful.''

''Insomnia?''

He shook his head. ''Not insomnia. A nightmare on two legs. I found an unexpected visitor in my apartment when I got up there.''

''You went out cruising? In the middle of the night? I thought you just closed up and went to bed.''

''I didn't go out anywhere. I found an unexpected visitor in my apartment when I got up there.''

Clarisse put down her knife and the portion of muffin she'd not yet eaten. Her expression was suddenly troubled. ''Someone broke in?''

''More or less.''

''Please, Val—details, not riddles.''

Valentine told her about finding Bander in his bedroom, their ensuing argument, and his forcibly ejecting the man from the building. He held back his having found the neckties hanging on the knob of the closet door.

''That's very upsetting,'' Clarisse said, tossing her napkin beside her plate. ''I think you should walk directly across the street and report that man. I'll go with you if you like.''

''What I'd like is another cup of coffee.''

Clarisse stared, taken aback.

Valentine leaned back in his chair. ''Clarisse, if I go to the police, what do you propose I tell them?''

''About that false repair call. About Bander deceiving you to gain entrance to your apartment. About his attacking you.''

"I told you, Bander covered his tracks as far as the repair call goes—and he actually did adjust the pilot light. The cops will ask one question—'Did you ever sleep with this guy before?' Answer? 'Yes.' End of questioning. They'll wink knowingly at each other and say, 'Lover's quarrel.' "

"But—"

"All right," Valentine said, "suppose they do question Bander. It's his word against mine."

Clarisse sat back and glanced disconcertedly out the window. "Do you think Bander pulls this sort of thing very often?"

"I think he's done it before. He had it down pat. What difference does it make?"

"Remember the Boston Strangler?" Clarisse asked quietly.

"We never tricked," said Valentine.

"When he was killing women in Boston, no one could ever describe him, and he didn't rely on makeup or a disguise."

"So?"

"He used something much better than a disguise. He wore repairman's overalls. Witnesses only remembered seeing a repairman going into the building—and most of them didn't even remember that. Repairmen are invisible. Bander wears a uniform. He can get into apartments day or night without any trouble."

"No. I'm ahead of you this time. Bander's unpleasant, and I don't like him, but I would not peg him for a psychopathic killer. Or I wouldn't, except for something I found this morning."

"What?"

Valentine told her about finding his neckties draped over the knob of his bedroom closet door.

"Oh, that," said Clarisse guiltily. "That was me."

"You? What were you doing in my bedroom?"

"I needed to borrow your tan webbed belt. You know how color coordination rules my life. Anyway, I forgot to put the ties back."

"That's a relief. I was about to compose an anonymous tip-off to the cops on Bander."

"I still think you should." She glanced at the clock. "I also think we ought to go for a walk in the neighborhood before this beautiful morning turns too hot."

Valentine swallowed the last of his coffee and pushed back his chair. "Good idea, and while we're at it, you can tell me about the vicarious thrill you got from rummaging around in my drawers—if you'll pardon the expression."

Clarisse groaned as she rolled her eyes. She snatched her sunglasses and keys from a table as they walked to the apartment door.

On the sidewalk outside they began to walk leisurely down Warren Avenue.

"Excuse me, but can I see you a minute, Valentine?" a male voice said behind Clarisse.

The couple turned around and saw a handsome uniformed policeman holding his hat in one hand and erasing sweat from his brow with the other. His hair was strikingly blond and wavy.

The policeman smiled at Clarisse in greeting, and she raised her glasses and looked him over. Lowering them back onto the bridge of her nose, she said, "You look just as good in uniform this morning as you did last night wearing cutoffs and a T-shirt in the bar."

The policeman's expression sobered markedly as he looked to Valentine for an explanation.

"I pointed out the plainclothesmen for her last night," Valentine explained to the man. "I really felt I had to."

"I keep secrets better than the dead," Clarisse put in. "I'm Clarisse Lovelace, by the way."

"Chester Arthur," the policeman said, and shook hands with her.

"Like the president," Clarisse replied, delighted.

"Yes, except I'm Chester *B*. Arthur." He put his hat back on. He took a moment before he spoke.

"You did want to talk to me?" Valentine prompted.

"It's about some of your customers—three of them in particular—who were at the talent show last night. A woman who calls herself B.J. and two men she's always running with."

"Ruder and Cruder," Valentine confirmed. "We know them."

"What can you tell me?"

"When I say we know them," Valentine confided, "I don't mean to imply they're friends. They're not. They're customers."

"Then what do you hear about them?"

"Heavy leather, heavy drugs, heavy action," Valentine said. "What you see is what you get."

"But the two guys *are* gay, right?"

"Of course," said Clarisse.

"But they run with a woman," the policeman insisted, not argumentatively but as if trying to reason it out.

"Some gay men will do the sort of things B.J. likes," Valentine continued, adding, "the sort of things straight men won't do."

The policeman nodded slowly, evidently trying to make some sense of it. "I just came from a little visit with B.J. At the South Mortuary. She made a positive ID on both her two playmates."

Valentine and Clarisse were completely taken aback by this revelation. Clarisse pulled off her glasses.

"They're dead?" Valentine asked. "*Both* of them?"

"Ruder and Cruder are dead?" Clarisse blurted out.

The policeman supplied them with the victims' real names. "They were strangled," he went on. "Neckties."

"What else is new in this town?" Clarisse snapped, shoving her glasses back over her eyes.

"They were at the talent show last night," Valentine said.

"And they were killed last night also," the policeman emphasized.

"Where were they killed?"

"Back Bay. Marlborough Street, between Fairfield and Gloucester. In a building undergoing renovation. A carpenter putting in overtime on the place found their bodies this morning. They were in separate rooms on the top floor—one in the back, one in the front.''

"Wait a minute," Clarisse interrupted. "Those two never wore neckties, and where do you find neckties in a building that's being renovated?''

"The murderer brought them with him," Valentine supplied calmly. "Am I right?" he asked the policeman.

"It looks like that's what might have happened.''

"Were there just two neckties used in the killing?" Clarisse inquired.

"Yes. Why?''

"Because other murder victims were practically hog-tied.''

"Were they handcuffed?" Valentine asked.

"How did you know?" said Chester B. Arthur, startled.

Valentine shrugged. "It makes sense. Ruder and Cruder wore handcuffs wherever they went.''

"What about B.J.," Clarisse demanded. "Where is she in all this?''

"Somewhere else," the policeman answered with deliberate vagueness.

"I'll just bet she has one interesting alibi," Clarisse remarked.

The policeman did not reply.

"That woman was always with Ruder and Cruder," Valentine said. "Always.''

"They were practically Siamese triplets," Clarisse added.

The policeman ignored their comments and asked instead, "In the bar last night, did either of you see them talk to anyone for any length? Someone they might have gotten together with?''

"The only thing I heard from them," Valentine said, "were orders for drinks.''

The officer looked to Clarisse. "I saw you have a little encounter with them over by the edge of the stage.''

"Yes, but it was hardly a conversation. If you'd been listening, you'd have heard sexual innuendo from them and a sharp retort from me. That's all.''

The policeman accepted this with a nod. He glanced toward the station house and then back to them.

"Just one more thing," he said to Valentine. "Were you here all night?"

"This is the first time I've been outside since the parade yesterday afternoon. Am I a suspect?"

The policeman forced an unconvincing smile of dismissal. "I have to get back. Thanks for your time."

Clarisse and Valentine watched the policeman in silence as he turned and walked back across the street.

chapter
twelve

AT FOUR O'CLOCK IN THE AFTERNOON IT WAS HOTTER than it had been at noontime. The sun beat mercilessly down on the shoppers in Boston's Downtown Crossing, the designated main shopping area of the city. The heat wilted the workers who were coming down from their air-conditioned offices. Teenagers from the suburbs, radios perched on shoulders, wandered about listlessly. Street vendors and sidewalk singers shouted in such garbled voices that it was impossible to tell what they were selling or singing. There was a salsa band, in full regalia, stationed in front of Jordan Marsh's bridal display window. A bag lady with a portable loudspeaker system in a small upright shopping cart was singing at full volume a medley of songs from *My Fair Lady*. Beneath the street, the Red and Orange Line subway trains rumbled and shook every fifteen seconds or so.

Clarisse stepped out from Filene's perfumed coolness into this cacophony of heat, noise, and odor. She was laden with packages from Filene's (upper store as well as basement), Waldenbooks, Capezio, Lane Bryant, and Woolworth's. She scanned the headlines of a street vendor's afternoon papers, trying to decide if any of the headlines were worth her putting down her packages to get at her purse, inaccessible beneath the pyramid of bundles she carried in front of her.

All the newspaper stories seemed to be political or criminal. Clarisse frowned and told herself that she'd had enough of crime and politics for the rest of the summer.

The two latest necktie killings, of Ruder and Cruder, would have made the front page of the *Boston Herald* had not a well-known Mormon pop singer chosen that particular day to announce her second divorce. But the deaths of the two men made the top of page three, where a full column was devoted to a simple listing of what the dead men were wearing. Everything seemed to have been fashioned either of leather or of steel. Even the relatively sober *Globe* pointed out the sadomasochistic tendencies of the two men, referred (though not by name) to B.J., and suggested that perhaps the previous deaths should also be looked at in the light of homosexual game playing. *Gay Community News*, caught between deadlines on its regular issues, came out with a special four-page edition decrying the inability of the Boston police to make any headway in the investigation into the murders. Several letters hinted darkly that the "reprehensible police inaction and gross inactivity" was a conspiracy against the gay community in retaliation against its recent political and economic progress. Channel 4 News very quickly started up a series of reports, airing at noon and eleven, on "Fear and Trembling in the Gay Community."

They interviewed Clarisse, presiding over a near-empty Slate. All this past week Slate's business seemed to be made up principally of reporters and plainclothesmen. Although there was a traditional summer outflux after Gay Pride Week, Clarisse knew that the murders were destroying business. It had been announced everywhere—on television and in the papers—that the double murder victims had last been seen in Slate. Everyone was also reminded that the other victims had been seen in the bar in the hours directly before their murders, as well.

Clarisse turned from the newsstand as three surburban teenagers stormed up the concrete steps from the subway, as if determined not to lose a minute's pleasure in the heart of the city. They collided with her, and she stumbled backward, only catching herself from falling by dropping all the packages at once.

The Filene's Basement bag split open, bottom to top, and fifteen pairs of patterned socks spilled out on the sidewalk. Three pairs of shoes from Lane Bryant fell out of their boxes and got mixed up with the socks. The four mystery novels she'd bought at Waldenbooks slid out of the plastic bag and were stepped on before she could gather them up. Dessert from the most expensive bakery on the street she gave up on altogether and kicked the chocolate Napoleon down the subway steps. Her Capezio leotard alone remained intact.

"Have I got everything?" she asked herself aloud, mentally checking off the packages.

"No," said a man's voice behind her.

She turned, and exclaimed, "Father!"

Father Cornelius McKimmon was holding her maroon purse out to her.

"Oh, thank God," she said, and extended a hand through the tattered remnant of the packages she held. Father McKimmon gave her the purse, and it disappeared into the pyramid again.

The priest wore black slacks and no suit coat but a short-sleeved black shirt with his white collar in place. His hair had been recently trimmed and was neatly combed. He was silent for a few moments but seemed disposed to linger, as if there were something he wanted to say to her.

Awkwardly shifting the packages in her arms once more, Clarisse asked, "What brings you into Boston today? Have you been to the men's shelter on Pine Street?"

"No," he replied. As he did, Clarisse surreptitiously breathed in and found not the slightest scent of liquor on his breath. "An old friend of mine died, and before he went, he asked me to officiate at his funeral mass. I'm on my way over to the shrine on Arch Street now.'' He made a gesture toward the opposite end of the pedestrian mall.

"Oh, I'm sorry."

"So am I. I'd planned to go up to Gloucester with a friend for the afternoon."

"I see," said Clarisse, taken aback for a moment. "Well, death does have a way of interfering with one's plans."

Father McKimmon took no apparent note of the irony in her voice. "The man who died wasn't a close friend," he explained. "Hardly a friend at all, really." He lowered his voice and said confidentially, "In fact, I couldn't stand him." He sighed. "But priests can't go through life ignoring last requests, can they?"

"I guess not," Clarisse said uncertainly as she rearranged her bundles once more and began to take her leave. "Niobe is expecting me any minute, Father, and—"

"Give her my best," he said quickly and with unexpected earnestness. "I haven't seen her lately, you know. I've been away."

Clarisse said nothing. She somehow had the feeling that she was going to find out where the priest had been whether she wanted to know or not. She was right.

"I was in Vermont. An old priory up there. Very quiet and peaceful, and compared to the city this time of year, very cool."

"Yes," said Clarisse. "I have a vague memory of what it was like to get away in the summer. Very vague."

"It wasn't a vacation. I was drying out," he added proudly. "The order that used to be in the priory disbanded some years ago. It's been turned into a center for the treatment of priests with alcoholic problems. The sisters have a place in New Hampshire."

Although surprised by Father McKimmon's casual revelation, Clarisse could not help asking, "Are there a lot of alcoholic nuns?" Her curiosity had overcome her desire to get to a place where she could put down the packages, which had begun to sag and slip in her perspiring hands.

"I've been up there for weeks," said the priest. "And I'll probably be going back. I'm really only in town for a couple of days. So give Niobe my best. Tell her I miss Slate."

"Thank you," said Clarisse with a sigh. "I wish I could say you're the only regular customer who's stopped coming to the bar."

"The murders?" he asked quietly, and Clarisse nodded. "I'm sorry to hear it," he said, "but I have to run now and send Tim's soul on its merry little way."

Now Father McKimmon seemed as anxious to be away from Clarisse as a moment ago he had seemed disposed to linger.

"Don't keep Tim waiting on my account," she said, unable to make anything of his sudden mood shift.

Father McKimmon smiled—distractedly, Clarisse thought—and turned off suddenly into the crowd.

"I WANT THE STORY," SAID CLARISSE TO NEWT. THEY were sitting with Niobe at the bar in Slate. "The *real* story on Father McKimmon." She took a sip of her wine cooler. The purchases she'd made at Downtown Crossing were stacked on the bar to her right. She picked idly at one torn bag. "There was something very odd about him today. He really went out of his way to tell me that he had gone to Vermont to dry out."

"It's part of the therapy," said Niobe definitely. "You tell everybody you're an alcoholic and that you've gone on the wagon so that the embarrassment factor works in your favor."

"The embarrassment factor?" echoed Clarisse.

"Yeah, when everybody knows you've giving it up, you're too embarrassed to be seen drinking," said Newt. "Pretty standard stuff."

"We're talking about the Roman Catholic church," said Clarisse. "They really encourage their priests to go around and announce to virtual strangers that they're alcoholic?"

"You're a bartender," said Niobe smoothly. "Father

111

McKimmon was warning you that if he ever got desperate and comes in here, you're to tell him no and encourage him to get out of harm's way.''

"I see," Clarisse said.

"You two think this is the only bar he knows about?" Newt smirked. "I've watched Father McKimmon hop up onto the wagon and then tumble off again like he was doing circus tricks. Don't get your hopes up. Believe me, soon enough you'll be sweeping him off the steps in the morning. He'll be going through the trash, swilling the dregs out of the bottles you toss out.''

"You always dredge up the worst things to say about him," Clarisse said. "Why do you dislike the man so much?"

Newt turned back toward the bar. "I don't dislike Father McKimmon," he said quietly, feigning innocence.

"He loathes him," Niobe corrected.

"Yes, but why?" Clarisse asked.

Newt didn't answer, but took a swallow of his beer.

"Come on, give over, kid.''

Newt sighed. "Are you really in the mood for human drama on such a hot afternoon?''

"If it's sordid enough," said Clarisse, brightening.

"Newt grew up in Malden," Niobe erupted with full verbal animation. "The product of a broken home. His father deserted hearth and home when Newt was nine years old, leaving him in the clutches of an alcoholic strumpet who went by the name of Mother. Malden, as you know, Clarisse, is the very same town where Father McKimmon's parish rests.''

"Niobe!" Newt protested. "You're making it sound like 'This Is Your Life.' I don't think Clarisse wants to hear about my puberty.''

Niobe stood up, offended. "I'm *so* sorry," she said huffily. Two overweight workmen wearing hard hats entered the bar and signaled to her for two Schlitzes.

"I went to parochial schools," Newt went on. "Kindergarten through high school. Boring. I was very athletic—basketball, soccer, gymnastics, etcetera. I went out for all sports because I was good at them and because it kept me away from home and Mommie Dearest and because I liked locker rooms. When I was a senior in high school, this new priest, Father Fiore, was assigned to the parish. He coached soccer, and he was also my academic adviser. He took a genuine interest in me. He tried to straighten my mother out. He came over to the house to have a talk with her, but she was soused and tried to slap the make on him.''

He took a long swallow of beer, finishing off his can. Clarisse reached over the bar and snagged another one out of the cooler for him. ''Go on,'' she said as she popped it open.

''Midterm of my senior year, a third priest was assigned to the parish. He was also attached to the high school as vice-principal. That third priest was Father Cornelius McKimmon. He was going to change the way things were done. He tried to ride herd over everyone—staff and students. No tact at all.''

''So what happened?''

''McKimmon was jealous of Fiore because he was so well liked. McKimmon, by the way, was also a closet queen. I picked that up right away. One night, when I was leaving basketball practice, I ran into him. He'd been drinking. He made a pass. I rejected him. The next week somebody made a couple of anonymous phone calls to the Cardinal's residence in Brookline. This caller accused Father Fiore of sexual misconduct with some of the school athletes. His Eminence the Cardinal managed to keep it pretty much under wraps, but a scandal is a scandal, and we were all dragged in and given the third degree. Jesuits invented the third degree, you know. Then suddenly one day Father Fiore was gone. Eventually he left the church.''

''You think Father McKimmon made those calls?''

''No,'' Newt returned flatly. ''There was this kid who *hadn't* rejected McKimmon's advances—he did it. McKimmon put him up to it.''

''How do you know that, Newt?''

''The kid told me—after I beat him to a pulp.''

113

"Did you say anything to anybody?"

"I tried," said Newt bitterly. "But of course they went directly to Corny about it, and you know what Corny said? He said that I was the main one that Fiore had corrupted. So then *I* got thrown out of school, too. Three weeks before graduation. Totally turned me off education. That's why I never went to college."

"Had you . . . ?"

"Had sex with Father Fiore?" Newt shook his head. "The man wasn't gay; that's one thing that made it so awful for him. I told you, he was a friend and was just trying to help me out."

Clarisse digested this a moment, then asked, "What's happened to McKimmon since then?"

"He's managed to rub everybody the wrong way. He was ambitious, but he drank too much. There were plenty of rumors about him, too, but nobody wanted another scandal linked to the parish, so they let him advance only up to a point. When he couldn't advance any more, he started to slide. He ended up getting work no one else wanted, like saying mass at the men's shelters. His parish now is fourth-rate and in the worst part of Malden."

"Okay, Newt," Clarisse said, "what happened back then was despicable, but that was nearly—what?—ten years ago?"

Newt turned on his stool and faced her. "Father McKimmon's a low-down son of a bitch. I know some guys he'd managed to lure into bed—with money I'll bet comes out of the poor box—and then these guys have lost their jobs. Some somebody called the places they worked and made insinuations and lies about their sexual habits."

"Why would Father McKimmon do that?"

"So he won't feel so ashamed about having to get drunk and pay somebody to have sex with. He turns things around and convinces himself his trick is the one who did something wrong. He erases his own guilt by screwing up other people's lives."

"Are you sure, Newt? Do you have proof?"

"I don't have tapes of the telephone calls, if that's what

you mean. But every one of those guys I know who lost their jobs had one thing in common—they'd carried on with Corny McKimmon and taken his money." Newt swiveled back to the bar and rested his elbow on the edge. "Every single one of them."

"These men," Clarisse said after a reflective moment, "who slept with Father McKimmon—"

"I didn't say they slept with him. They were just 'with' him, that's all."

"They were good friends of yours?"

"Some."

"Would I know any of them? I mean, are they still in Boston?"

"Most of 'em."

"Customers who come in here?"

"Some of them do; some of them *did*."

Clarisse looked at him sharply. "What do you mean— *did*?"

"Until they were murdered."

Clarisse's brow furrowed. "Who?"

"Jed Black. He took money from Corny for sex a couple of times."

"What?" Clarisse blurted. "*Jed* took money?"

"It was five or six years ago, when Jed was a student and living in this slummy rooming house on the wrong side of Beacon Hill."

"I see. Who else?"

"Remember the Shrimp? The smallest cowboy in the world with the nastiest mouth?"

"*He* fooled around with Father McKimmon?"

Newt shrugged. "He bragged about it. Said it was kinky to do it with a priest. He didn't even get paid."

"You're making all this up, aren't you?"

"No, I'm not," said Newt staunchly.

"You realize what you're implying, don't you—about Father McKimmon and the necktie murders, I mean?"

"I'd be a fool not to realize it."

"Have you told any of this to the police?"

"You know what they'd say? First thing they'd say is,

115

he's a priest and priests don't commit murder. Second thing they'd say is 'You're trying to get back at him because he had you thrown out of school.' Third thing they'd say is 'Hey, you knew all these dead guys, and you went to bed with 'em, didn't you?' "

"Did you?" asked Clarisse.

"Unfortunately," he said quietly.

"The number of men in this town that Newt *hasn't* gone to bed with," said Niobe, passing by on her way to the cash register, "you could count on the fingers of one maimed hand."

Clarisse was silent a moment. Then she asked, "How does McKimmon manage not to get defrocked?"

Newt grunted a laugh. "Like I said, Father McKimmon is one sneaky son of a bitch. Until now, didn't you think he was just this harmless priest right out of some Forties' Bing Crosby movie who just happened to have a little drinking problem?"

Clarisse admitted he was right.

"He had you fooled, too."

"Whatever happened to your mother?" she asked suddenly.

Newt averted his eyes and said quietly, "My mother committed suicide."

"Oh, Newt," Clarisse said, greatly distressed. "I—"

"That is not true!" Niobe cried indignantly, on her way back to the hard hats with change. "Clarisse, Newt's mother runs a broken-down chicken ranch in the back-woods of Appalachia! Nine years ago she just woke up one day, drew all her money out of the bank, bought a used camper, and just drove away. She ended up in Kentucky, and that's where she is today." Niobe swiped at Newt's shoulder with the back of her hand. "You stop telling people your mother offed herself!" She shot a sidewise glance at Clarisse, still swiping at a now dodging Newt. "Honestly, he'll make up a story about anything, and it all sounds real!"

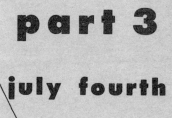

part 3

july fourth

chapter
thirteen

AT A QUARTER TO EIGHT ON THE EVENING OF JULY Fourth, a taxi pulled to a stop mid-block on Beacon Street between Exeter and Fairfield streets. The back door banged open, and Clarisse, struggling with an enormous glass bowl covered with plastic wrap, lurched up out of the backseat. She angled her hip smartly against the door and slammed it shut. Giving a toss of her hair to get a wayward wave out of one eye, she took a breath and dashed through a break in traffic across to the Charles River side of the street. She collided with a group of laughing young women carrying blankets, radios, and six-packs, regained her precarious balance, and hurried up the stoop of a brownstone. She carefully backed through the outside door into the foyer.

Clarisse balanced the chilled bowl precariously in the crook of one arm while she used her free hand to punch the button under the end mailbox. The identifying label on the mailbox read: "N. Feng—*not* Newton." The mailbox next to it was labeled "Newt Newton." On the day after a marital rift noticeably more violent than the one that had preceded it, Niobe had announced in a voice of doom she was moving out of the apartment and Newt's life forever. She made a great production of bag packing and immediate division of property. The next day, Niobe kept her promise and moved out—into the apartment directly above. Newt claimed that she caused the fight just because she wanted a better view and a whole bathroom for herself, but Niobe claimed that the apartment coming available that morning was a fluke of fate. Although friends of the couple repeatedly pointed out to her that her action could hardly be construed as a true separation, Niobe claimed that the politics of her action far outweighed its illogicality.

As Clarisse awaited a reply over the house intercom, she looked up and down Beacon Street. Knots of people with blankets and picnic baskets and plastic coolers were making their way toward the Esplanade. At sundown the Boston Pops would begin its annual Independence Day concert on the banks of the Charles River. As usual, the crowd was predicted to be in the hundreds of thousands. Soft twilight deepened the shadows between the elms and lindens bordering the sidewalks. Amplified music, rock mostly, underscored the parties in progress up and down both sides of the street. Exploding firecrackers echoed every few seconds, and an occasional Roman candle, launched from a rooftop, made a bright streak in the slowly darkening sky.

"That better be Clarisse with the lobster salad," came Niobe's voice over the intercom. "Confucius say: No eat/ No greet."

"Clarisse say: If you think that I spent two hours murdering innocent crustaceans so that I could make small talk over an intercom, you've got another think coming, sister. It doesn't rhyme, but I trust you get the message."

The latch buzzed immediately, and Clarisse pushed her way through the heavy oak door. She trudged up the stairs to the sixth floor, realizing for the first time in her life just how heavy a bowl of lobster salad could be.

Niobe's apartment door was ajar. On the door itself was a gaily painted image of the Laughing Buddha. Niobe had taped tiny paper American flags into his upturned palms.

Clarisse edged the door open with the side of her foot and kicked it closed once she was inside. Clarisse walked the length of the narrow hallway connecting all the rooms of the apartment without finding anyone. Just before she reached the kitchen, however, she heard Valentine's laughter from above. The skylight was open, and the collapsible ladder had been attached. Clarisse shoved her bowl of lobster salad onto a refrigerator shelf already crowded with containers of prepared food. She took a bottle of Grolsch from a door rack, a glass from a shelf, and carefully mounted the flimsy ladder to the cedar roof deck.

Newt took the bottle and glass from Clarisse, and she was able to negotiate the sharp metal lip of the skylight without doing much more than snagging a thread in her brand-new pair of pleated linen trousers. Standing near a hibachi and wearing a white chef's apron and a too large chef's hat, Newt wielded a greasy metal spatula. Valentine and Niobe stood at the low ledge at the back of the building's roof, looking out over the Esplanade and the Charles River.

A radio on the corner of the ledge was tuned to one of the stations that would broadcast the Pops Concert live. A soft-voiced female announcer, stationed on the roof of a building two or three numbers down, was describing the scene from very nearly the same perspective. The riverbank for a mile in either direction was a sea of people lounging on blankets or cross-legged on towels. The crowd was most dense just in front of the Hatch Shell, where the white-jacketed musicians were setting up. The river itself was filled with boats—yachts, rowboats, rubber rafts, sunfish, and nearly anything that stood a pretty good chance of staying afloat for a few hours. Traffic had been closed on Storrow Drive, and the six lanes were nearly rush-hour busy with strollers, skaters, skateboarders, bicyclists, and joggers.

Valentine and Niobe were staring out over the crowd with matching binoculars.

"Don't everybody jump up and down, cheer, wave, and generally risk falling over the edge in euphoria over my arrival," Clarisse announced as Newt poured her Grolsch out into a glass.

"Here's to the twilight's last gleaming," he said as he handed her the beer and reached for a swallow of his own drink.

"Glad you could make it," said Valentine over his shoulder. He immediately turned back toward the crowd with his binoculars.

"Make yourself comfortable," said Niobe—but she didn't even turn around.

"Thanks," said Clarisse, giving up. She stood beside Newt at the grill and watched him fan the glowing coals with a folded section of newspaper. Next to the hibachi a round table was covered with a red-and-white checkered tablecloth and laden with plates, the Newton-Feng wedding silverware, embroidered napkins, a silver ice bucket, and several bottles of liquor, mixers, and glasses. On an enormous tray close at hand was a bountiful display of cubed beef and lamb and a variety of vegetables for shish kebab. Skewers with brass finials in the shape of pineapples were laid out in a fan shape next to the tray.

"How were things at the bar when you left?" Newt asked. "Pretty empty, I bet. Probably everybody's on the river tonight."

"It was pretty quiet," replied Clarisse. "Sean said he didn't mind being left alone. When the concert's over, I'll run back and help him with the postfireworks mob."

"Be careful," said Newt. "Not only is it Fourth of July, but it's the full moon."

"Here's one!" Valentine exclaimed suddenly.

"Oh, God, where? Where?" demanded Niobe, scanning the crowd with her binoculars.

"Just leaving Back Street," Valentine reported, "crossing Storrow Drive at Exeter."

Clarisse shot Newt a questioning glance. He answered with an elaborate roll of his eyes.

"Oh, God!" cried Niobe, "there she is. I see her! I see her! She's the best one yet!"

"I'm almost afraid to ask what they're up to," Clarisse said to Newt as she took a swallow of the dark beer.

"They're looking for the fattest person wearing the tightest outfit in Boston tonight."

"Oh, God," cried Niobe ecstatically, "three hundred twenty-five pounds if she's an ounce, and horizontal stripes."

"And wearing a Walkman. I love her," said Valentine with low-voiced reverence. "Oh! Did you see? She just knocked over a kid on a racing bike."

"Total style," said Niobe.

"They've been doing that for the last hour," Newt confided to Clarisse.

"You mean I took two hours off work, leaving Sean to take care of the bar on the Fourth of July, and schlepped a bowl of lobster salad all the way across town to be subjected to *this*? What happened to sensible pastimes, like Trivial Pursuit and getting drunk and viciously gossiping about all your friends?"

"Valentine's got the eyes of an eagle," Niobe said admiringly, putting her binoculars down with a sigh. "It's getting dark. I'm going to get the candles." She slipped easily over the raised lip of the skylight and started down the ladder.

"Niobe?" Newt called down the opening. "Start handing the food up to me. The concert's going to start in a little while, and I don't want to cook during the whole thing. While you're at it, bring up more beer and a bottle of soda water."

"You are *not* my lord and master, Newt!" Niobe shouted from below.

"I am until the divorce is legally finalized," he sing-songed back.

"I'll go help her," Clarisse offered and got up. She climbed down the ladder, leaving the two men alone.

Valentine put his binoculars aside. From below he could hear the mingling of conversation with the clinking of ice against glass. He moved aside one of several potted geraniums lined up along the parapet and looked over the edge.

The fire escape zigzagging down the apartment building was filling up as people climbed out of the windows of the lower floors. A blonde woman directly below caught sight of Valentine and smiled up alluringly. Valentine returned the gesture and then withdrew from sight. He joined Newt at the hibachi.

Newt was skewering the meat. The blood of the raw beef and pork stained his hand and sizzled in the hot coals. Valentine dropped several ice cubes into his glass and looked all around. In the direction away from the river, light from the street lamps made a lacelike illumination through the trees. Many of the rooftops of the buildings to their right and left and across the street were crowded with people, and Newt's wasn't the only barbecue going. Roman candles erupted from rooftops deeper in Back Bay. The warm-up sounds of the Pops were emitted tinnily from dozens of radios throughout the area.

"What's the matter?" Newt asked suddenly. "Thinking patriotic thoughts?"

Valentine glanced back over his shoulder at the jagged rooftops silhouetted against the clear night sky. "Actually, I was thinking about the last necktie murders—those two leather numbers who were friends of B.J."

"What about them?"

"Which building were they killed in? Can you see it from up here?"

Newt aimed a skewer of beef and onion to his left. "Next block down, other side of the street, fourth house in from the corner. You can see it when the trees are bare."

Valentine looked in the direction Newt had pointed. "Are they still working on renovating that building?"

"Oh, sure. As soon as the cops gave the go-ahead, the carpenters and electricians were back in there. A friend of mine's on the work crew."

"Really? Did he say anything to you about it?"

"He wasn't the one who found the bodies, if that's what you mean."

"No," said Valentine, "but was there blood or anything?"

"He said that the one found in the front room had uri-nated when he was killed, but that was all. Urine doesn't make much of a stain, by the way. He said they were lucky it wasn't a stabbing, because they'd have had to rip up part of the floor. He said that the place smelled to high heaven, though."

"Smelled. From what? Their bodies hadn't been in there long enough to decompose, and urine can't make *that* much of an odor."

"He said it was some sort of chemical smell. It was some liquid that had been spilled on the floor and in some of the insulation near one of the bodies."

"Chemical," Valentine repeated thoughtfully. "Amyl nitrate?"

Newt shrugged. "That's what I figured, because my friend is straight. He wouldn't know poppers if you spilled them in his shirt pocket."

"You know a straight man?" Valentine asked.

"Somebody has to befriend them."

"Did your friend have anything else interesting to say?"

Newt looked up and thrust out his right arm, displaying a chrome-studded black leather wristband. Valentine looked from it up to Newt.

"Newt, you're not going to tell me your friend found that and gave it to you instead of to the police."

"Yep. The cops missed it. It was caught in that insula-tion where the chemical smell was." Newt held his arm up and looked at the bracelet. "I never owned anything that belonged to a murdered person before. I used to have a suicide jacket but never a murder victim's jewelry."

"That could be evidence," Valentine said seriously.

"Daniel, those two weren't strangled with leather wrist-bands, for God's sake. Nobody'll ever miss it. Every time I put this on, I'll think of poor old Ruder."

Valentine knitted his brow. "How do you know it be-longed to Ruder and not Cruder?"

"I don't, but I always thought Ruder was the better looking. If I'm going to wear something that belonged to a murder victim, I like to think it was worn by a reasonably good looking murder victim.''

Valentine took a swallow of his drink. "You know, Newt," he said quietly, "there's no way of knowing for sure who that wristband belonged to."

Newt lowered his arm. "What do you mean?"

"Maybe it didn't belong to the victim. Maybe it belonged to the murderer. It could have come off in a struggle."

Newt gazed at the wristband with disturbed, renewed interest. "I didn't think of that . . ."

"It could have had the killer's fingerprints on it."

Newt turned the bracelet about his wrist. "It's got my fingerprints all over it now."

"And if the murderer realizes it's missing and he sees it on your wrist . . ."

Clarisse thrust herself unexpectedly up through the skylight. Valentine gave her an arm up and over the lip of the opening.

"Okay, you two, form a line to the right."

Clarisse repeatedly leaned back down and up again as she took and passed on an enormous ceramic bowl of potato salad, lobster salad, Boston baked beans, a mop bucket full of ice and beer, two hot spinach quiches, and a covered bowl of rice and tomatoes.

The first strains of "The Star Spangled Banner" came from the radio. An enormous cheer welled up from the half million people gathered within a mile radius of the Hatch Shell.

The moment was oddly solemn. The four friends stood on the deck, looking out over the river and the standing crowd, and Valentine just managed to resist his Eagle Scout impulse to put his hand over his heart, for at that moment he caught sight—and scent—of Newt's new leather wristband, charring among the coals of the hibachi.

chapter
fourteen

At nine-thirty the Boston Pops began the *1812 Overture*, the traditional prelude leading to the fabled fireworks display that would light up the entire Charles River Basin. Valentine, Clarisse, Newt, and Niobe sat in director's chairs lined up along the back ledge of the deck facing the river. Now they were all on coffee and liqueurs. They sipped their drinks contentedly and listened to Tchaikovsky's music pouring from the radio on the floor behind them—and from every rooftop and through every open window all around.

Niobe had brought up the small cage containing her canary, Rodan, and fed it shreds of charred pork through the narrow bars. The cage now rested on her lap, though every now and then it jiggled with a sudden violent movement of the bird inside. Niobe looked to her left at the profiled faces.

"I'll bet the police arrest B.J. before the week's out," she said.

The three profiles turned full face toward her.

"What brought that on?" Clarisse asked curiously.

Niobe shrugged. "I was just thinking about Ruder and Cruder getting killed in that house up the street. Every time I walk down Beacon past that place on my way to work or to the market or the library, I think about them."

"Just what is it you do think?" Valentine asked.

Niobe shifted in her chair to face the three of them. "I'm not one to waste tears on the gladly departed, but B.J. slept with 'em, ate with 'em, partied till she dropped with 'em."

"What are you getting at, Niobe?" Clarisse asked.

"After what's happened to those two, don't you think B.J. would show *some* sign of remorse? Maybe a few hot tears and convulsions? Oh, no, not that one."

"I didn't know you'd honed your talons today, Niobe," Newt said.

Niobe swiped casually at her husband with the back of her hand but otherwise ignored his interruption. "You know what B.J. did after the cops got done questioning her? She went straight from the cops over to Innovations in Leather. She had herself fitted out head to toe in a brand-new black leather outfit. Made 'em do the alterations while she stood there. They won't usually do that, but B.J.'s such a good customer of theirs."

"She calls that outfit her widow's hides," Newt put in, and again jerked back from Niobe's swatting hand.

"Leather or crepe, Niobe," Clarisse said, "a mourning ensemble is a mourning ensemble."

"So B.J. got this outfit," Niobe pressed on, "then called up her dealer and ordered about nine pounds of blow."

"A gram," Newt corrected.

"Shut up, Newt!" Niobe cried.

"I would like to hear the point of this story before we get the cannons and the bells," Valentine announced.

"B.J. coked herself beyond recognition. She climbed into a cab and went off to Metro, where she danced herself into a sweaty mess and drank her face off. Then," Niobe sputtered with indignation, "then she came back across town, picked up five men, and dragged them back to her apartment for the night. That is how she demonstrated her supposed grief at losing her supposed two best friends in the whole world. Is that woman a petrified cookie or what?''

''Well''—Clarisse blinked—''maybe that really was B.J.'s way of working out her grief.''

Niobe gave Clarisse a look of totally disgusted disbelief. ''Are you taking EST training behind our backs?''

''You still haven't explained why you think B.J. might be arrested. The police questioned her and let her go.''

Niobe sat back hard. ''Because on every other night those two men were like flies and B.J. the flypaper. But not *that* night. Why?''

''She had a date that night,'' Newt said offhandedly.

''Newt, you know as well as I do that Ms. B.J. never goes on a date; she goes on *dates*.''

''Just because you don't approve of B.J.'s manner of mourning her dead is no reason to suspect her of murder,'' Clarisse pointed out.

''B.J. lets people see what she wants them to see,'' Newt said. ''You don't know how upset she was when Ruder and Cruder died. You don't have any idea, Niobe.''

Niobe looked at him coldly. ''I think she killed them. I think the three of them were in on the necktie murders. I'll bet Ruder and Cruder were getting cold feet and B.J. was afraid they'd squeal so she had to kill them.''

''Really?'' Valentine said calmly. ''What brilliant motive have you thought up for their committing the murders in the first place? Drug-induced blood lust? Kinks and kicks?''

''Something like that.''

''Niobe,'' Valentine went on, ''don't you think the cops would have figured that out right away? It's very hard for a killer who's stone-cold sober to murder somebody and get away without leaving any clues. But three killers who are always on drugs? And they haven't left a single usable clue?''

Niobe pushed out her lower lip in a pout as she turned away from Valentine.

Radios all over the neighborhood were turned up suddenly when the orchestra came in with the return of the

Marseillaise theme marking the beginning of the climax of the "1812."

"How do you know B.J. had a date on that night her two friends were murdered?" Niobe demanded suddenly of Newt.

"It's common gossip," Newt answered evenly.

"No, it isn't," Niobe challenged quickly. "I'd know. So would Valentine and Clarisse. You didn't know it, did you?"

Valentine and Clarisse shook their heads.

"*I* was B.J.'s date that night," Newt said flatly.

Valentine and Clarisse exchanged an uncomfortable glance at hearing this revelation. Niobe's features realigned into a flickering expression of hurt that swiftly changed to anger.

"Are you telling me . . ." Niobe began slowly.

Newt took a swallow of his liqueur. "If you launch into your naive-wife routine, I'm going to barf."

"You slept with B.J.?" Niobe went on. "You . . . you did it with her? A woman?"

"Stop calling it *it*. We made love."

"He's throwing it in my face!" Niobe screeched, gripping the arms of her chair. "He betrayed me with—a woman!"

"You brought the subject up, Niobe, not me."

Niobe jumped up, and Rodan's cage spilled onto the deck, with a small riot of squawking and yellow feathers. Niobe ran back to the table and feverishly mixed herself a very large gin and tonic.

"What in the world were you doing with B.J. that night?" Valentine asked Newt quietly and, he hoped, out of Niobe's earshot.

"What most men and women do when they climb into the sack together. Plus a few other items that aren't on the standard menu."

"No, I meant—"

"How long has this been going on?" Niobe demanded as she returned to her chair. She sat down hard. Over the radio the music was pounding toward the grand finale—the

Russians beating back the French with ferocity. Rodan's cage still lay on its side; an orange beak stuck up through the bars as if gasping for air.

"Just one little, innocent date," Newt explained. "That was it."

"You're lying!" cried Niobe huskily. "I know when you're lying!"

"Oh, Christ, Niobe." Newt sighed wearily. "I don't know why you're so upset."

"Were you with her the whole night?" Valentine ventured.

Clarisse jabbed him with her elbow. "Val!"

"This is adultery, Newt!" Niobe charged, backhanding him across his chest with the hand that fortunately was not grasped around her drink. "I can't believe you did this to me. I can't believe you cheated on me with B.J. I am not going to be married to a bisexual. I absolutely refuse—"

"Oh, God, Niobe, you and I haven't slept together in three and a half years. How can you still be jealous of anybody? It's your damned possessiveness that ruined our marriage in the first place. No wonder I screwed around so much behind your back. I'm surprised you haven't accused me of rubbing out Ruder and Cruder so that I could have B.J. all to myself."

"I wouldn't be a bit sur—"

Niobe's accusation was cut off.

From the riverbank below came the climax of the *1812*, with multiple explosions of powerful howitzers and the pealing of bells in every church tower in Back Bay and on Beacon Hill. The black sky above was suddenly and brightly illuminated by a brilliant volly of red, white and blue fireworks. Half a million people rose to their feet cheering and screaming.

Niobe and Newt, in their anger with one another, rose and faced off. Newt took a step forward, kicking Rodan's cage, which still lay on the deck between them. In a gesture of protectiveness, Niobe snatched up the cage—but snatched so violently that the brass handle snapped off and the cage flew out of her grasp.

It would have struck Newt in the face had he not knocked it aside with a sweep of his hand. Rodan's cage smashed against the brick parapet and broke into pieces.

Rodan, a fat little ball of yellow, staggered on the deck for a moment, then rose up on inexperienced wings. He whirled away, his chirping triumph echoed by cannon and carillon.

chapter fifteen

THURSDAY AFTERNOON WAS WARM, THE SMOOTH CERU-
lean sky marred only by a few drifting swatches of cloud.
Clarisse left her apartment carrying a brown canvas tote
bag with hand straps and walked with quick steps and clear
determination to the subway on Arlington Street. Once un-
derground, she boarded a Green Line train destined for
Government Center. When she emerged from the station
on the edge of City Hall Plaza, her eyes skimmed down
the line of businesses across the way and stopped at the
large plate-glass facade of the Universal Women's Health
Spa. The name was flourished in black script across the
glass, and between the words Clarisse could see Newt. He
wore a karate robe with a brown belt and was engaged in
animated conversation with three seriously overdressed
women. Clarisse glanced behind her in the direction of
busy Faneuil Hall Market Place as if trying to decide if
that wouldn't be a better destination. She looked back to
the health spa and drew a sharp breath as she saw the three
women exiting the place with loud farewells to Newt. He
held the door for them but was looking directly at Clarisse.

Clarisse made a disconcerted clucking sound at having been caught in her indecisive mode and left the curb. She waited for a break in traffic on Cambridge, but as none came, she dashed across anyway.

Newt was still holding the door to the spa when she came up to him.

"I thought that was you over there. Couldn't make up your mind between visiting a friend and gorging yourself at the market, right?" Newt let go of the door as he stepped back inside behind Clarisse.

The lobby was small, with white walls and moss-green carpeting. Small potted plants stood in the corners, and the walls were hung with lithographs of orchids. Soft rock music played over a speaker system, and distantly, from down the hallway, Clarisse could hear the stern voice of a female aerobics instructor. Behind the reception desk sat a young blonde woman with a peculiar orange/mahogany tan that was obviously the result of a tanning booth rather than the sun. She wore a pale lavender body stocking and iridescent green leg warmers. She was having a fight with a friend on the telephone and doodling in the appointment book.

"Sorry about the display last night," Newt apologized. "But after you two left, things really got going. Niobe threw three pots of geraniums at me. Then she attacked me with the leftover food. It all went over the side of the building onto the neighbors who were on the fire escape. They got drenched. Six of 'em came charging up to Niobe's apartment, screaming for blood. They left gobs of your lobster salad and baked beans all over the stairs and landing. What a mess."

"Sounds like Val and I missed the *real* fireworks of the evening."

"Why are you here?" Newt asked bluntly.

Clarisse reached into the pocket of her blouse and pulled out a newspaper clipping. Before she'd even unfolded it, Newt cried, "Great! You're going to take advantage of our July special."

"That's six so far," said the receptionist, pausing only a moment in her telephone conversation.

Newt took a step backward, and looked Clarisse up and down. "Not an ounce of fat on you. You're in great shape, unless you camouflage well, that is. Of course, we can help keep you that way."

Clarisse smiled at the flattery. "Actually, it's not keeping in shape that I'm so concerned about but—"

"God!" cried the receptionist, banging down the receiver. "Don't ever say that! You say that and the next thing you know you've got hips by Hindenburg. I see it all the time. Keeping in shape should be a total obsession."

"Millie," Newt cut in, "don't you have to update the appointment book or something?" He looked up at Clarisse and then began to speak in a quick, rehearsed voice: "I have to tell you that the free introductory visit is designed to give you an overall view of what we do here at the Universal Women's Health Spa. You'll have the opportunity to speak with our in-house diet and nutrition counselor, watch a videotaped lecture on basic human female anatomy, have a session—if you would like—with one of our excellent and expertly qualified physical-encounter instructors about tailoring an exercise program to your body needs and psychological desires, and then we have arranged for you to partake of an actual twenty-five-minute aerobics exercise class, after which you may enjoy the use of either our redwood sauna, steam room, or whirlpool bath. We will even be pleased to provide you proper attire."

Clarisse held up her tote. "Always prepared," she said. "But Newt, it's not the exercise program that interests me so much as the course *you* teach. Street defense? What do you call it exactly?"

"KMT," interjected Millie.

"What?"

"Kill, maim, and torture," Millie said with a grin.

Newt shot Millie a sour look and then said to Clarisse, "It's called 'Urban Street Defense for the Modern Woman.' I have another class in half an hour. We'll be working on basic moves, and you shouldn't have much trouble following if you want to give it a try."

"Yes, I would," said Clarisse.

"The muggers been after you?" Millie asked.

"No"—Clarisse shook her head—"I just think I ought to know how to *really* take care of myself."

"Smart, smart girl," Newt said as he tightened the belt on his kimono.

Ten minutes later, Clarisse emerged from a dressing room wearing a black body-stocking and gray leg warmers. Her hair was gathered at the nape of her neck with a metal clasp. She walked to the end of the hallway and entered an exercise room. Nine similarly dressed women were already waiting there, and Newt stood at the far end before a metal table where he was placing a cassette tape into a large portable player.

Clarisse looked about. The ceiling was soundproofed, and all four walls were covered floor to ceiling with mirror. She smiled at the nine other women—most appeared to be about her age or a little older, but they came in a variety of shapes and sizes.

Newt punched a few buttons, and characterless rhythmic music with a strong, slow, steady beat poured out of the speakers.

"Okay," Newt barked, "line up. Two rows, five in each. Lovelace, get rid of those leg warmers, and you there—in the pink—shed the scarf. We're not here for a fashion show."

After both women complied with his order, Newt went on: "Okay—warm-ups. Run in place!" He demonstrated and kept up his patter in time to the music: "Well, come on, ladies, let's get those knees in the air. The best defense is not to be there in the first place, but if you're in that dark alley, if you're in that deserted supermarket aisle, if you're on that empty subway platform and you have a chance to run, then do it. Run, run away, run away *fast*—you are running for your life. Run! Run! Run!"

"Run!" shouted the women as they pumped their fists into the air.

After ten minutes of warm-ups, Newt called Clarisse

over. "This is my friend Clarisse," he announced. "She's going to help with today's demonstration."

"But Newt, I can't. I don't know—"

"Don't worry," he reassured her quietly. "I'll take you through every step." Keeping his back to the class, he retrieved something from a black canvas gym bag in the corner. He held the object behind his back as he returned to Clarisse's side.

Newt pulled his arm around and opened his hand dramatically. A brown wool necktie unfurled from his hand. He handed it to Clarisse "Take it," he said.

"Why?"

"Because I want you to attack me with it, of course."

"Newt, *really*," Clarisse said, aghast, "this is a bit much."

Newt thrust the necktie into her hand.

"With the movements I'm going to show you today," Newt said to the class, "it would be virtually impossible for a would-be attacker to get the better of you. The main thing is not to panic, and remember what I'm going to show you. Okay, Clarisse, come at me. Try to subdue me. Do your best." Newt turned his back to Clarisse. The rest of the women in the room watched Clarisse expectantly. She shrugged, made fists, and pulled the long ends of the fabric taut. She advanced swiftly and looped the tie around Newt's neck, crossed the ends, and jerked them hard.

In one lightning gesture Newt threw his head down, shot both elbows straight back, raised one bent leg, and kicked backwards, slamming his calf against Clarisse's left leg. Clarisse took the elbows in her stomach as she lost her footing, released the tie, and crashed sideways to the mat. Newt darted cleanly away, the ends of the tie now loosely draped over his shoulders.

"Easy," he concluded, going back to give Clarisse a hand to get up. "You mustn't be afraid of losing your balance and falling with your attacker. I'll do it once more with Clarisse, only in slow motion, then we'll all try it."

After a second demonstration, Newt passed out ties. The women divided into pairs, taking turns to practice the maneuver. As Newt observed and gave points, advice, and approval to each pair of women, Clarisse still stared at the brown wool necktie draped loosely about his neck.

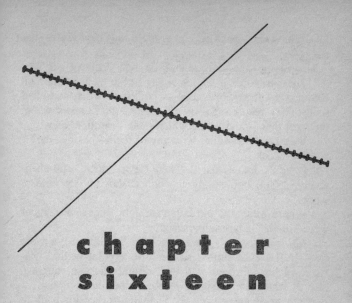

chapter
sixteen

EXHAUSTED AND SWEATING, CLARISSE SAT CROSS-LEGGED on the carpeted floor of the exercise room. The other participants had departed for the locker room, showers or sauna. Newt, arms folded, leaned against a table.

"Are you up for the course?"

With a laugh, Clarisse croaked, "You should call this course 'Advanced Masochistic Techniques for the Suicidal.' I enjoyed it, and I learned a lot, and now I just have to see if I can work it into my schedule." Clarisse took a breath and then said, "How long have you been sleeping with B.J.?"

Newt unfolded his arms. "That's why you really came here today, isn't it?"

"Yes," Clarisse replied bluntly, "I have a curious nature."

"What difference does it make to you who I do or don't sleep with?"

Clarisse didn't answer that question directly. "The police were at Slate today. They asked Valentine and me a lot of questions about B.J. Your name was mentioned—but not by us.''

Newt looked at Clarisse as if he didn't believe her.

''They asked us if we knew any of the men—other than Ruder and Cruder, of course—whom B.J. had gone to bed with. They reeled off a list of names—God knows where they got them—and asked which ones Valentine knew.''

''Was Daniel familiar with any of them—besides me?''

''Jed Black.''

''I didn't know that.'' Then Newt added, apprehensively, ''You don't want the police showing up here at work.''

''Where were you and B.J. that night Ruder and Cruder were killed?'' Clarisse persisted.

''My apartment,'' Newt answered quickly. ''We were just—'' His eyes shifted suddenly to a point behind Clarisse. In the mirrored wall to her right Clarisse caught a blur of white just outside the door of the room.

Newt stood away from the table and turned his back to Clarisse. He ejected the cassette tape from the player. ''Discussion is over,'' he said coldly. ''If the police want to ask me questions, I'll answer them, but don't think I'll let you dig into my private life so it can get back to Niobe.''

''I wouldn't do that, Newt, and you know it.''

''You honestly want me to believe you're prying just out of idle curiosity?''

''Yes,'' said Clarisse firmly. ''What time did B.J. leave your apartment?''

''You think B.J. killed Ruder and Cruder?'' Newt asked quietly.

''It's an obvious question.''

''I don't know what time B.J. left.''

''Well, was it late? Early? What?''

Newt shrugged. ''All I know is I was alone when I woke up.''

''What time did you two go to bed?''

''Clarisse, I don't punch a clock when I'm having sex,'' said Newt irritably. ''I don't know what time it was, but it was still dark when I went to sleep, and B.J. was still with me then. It was light when I woke up, and B.J. was gone. That's all there is to tell, okay? Why don't you leave now?''

Newt didn't look at her as he walked swiftly out of the room. Clarisse stared after him and then knit her brow when she detected movement in the crack of the open door. Someone was moving out from behind it. Clarisse got up and crossed to the doorway just in time to see a woman wearing a turban of white terry cloth and a second white towel wrapped around her body dart across the hall. Clarisse briefly saw the woman's profile as she disappeared into the locker room.

Although her hair was covered and she was not in her usual costume, Clarisse was certain the woman was B.J.

Clarisse crossed hurriedly into the locker room. The woman was nowhere to be seen.

Several of the women from Newt's self-defense course chatted idly and laughed as they finished dressing, while others moved about on the other side of the room in the steam-clouded shower stalls. Clarisse passed down a row of lockers past the stalls and looked into a short hallway leading to the steam room. The metal door of the room was closed, and the small window to the right of it was fogged over, but the interior was illuminated by a murky yellowish light. Clarisse opened the door of the steam room and stepped inside. She held the door ajar behind her until her eyes adjusted to the uneven play of light on the clouding mist. There seemed to be human shapes along the bench against the back wall, but when she could finally distinguish the depth of the room, these proved to be only shadows, and Clarisse realized that she was quite alone.

In turning to leave, Clarisse let go the door. It snapped shut with a click of the latch.

Clarisse pushed her hand against the metal door. It would not give. She swiftly traced her hand down one side in search of a handle. There was none. Clarisse pressed both palms flat against the hot, sweating metal and shoved hard at it, but the door was unmovable despite the force she exerted. She went over to the small pane of glass and wiped vapor from it. She saw no one in the exterior hall, and a bend in the angle of it prevented her seeing into the locker room. Clarisse shouted and banged her fist against the glass.

Steam hissed louder, and the room grew more oppressively humid. Mist thickened. Clarisse stepped back to the door and banged her fists against it. She kicked the door. It rattled but would not give.

The door flew unexpectedly open, and a startled Clarisse tumbled out into the arms of Millie, the receptionist.

"What the hell—" Millie exclaimed

Clarisse pulled back and took a deep gasp of cool air. She pushed aside her lank wet hair and then pressed her face into her upturned hands.

"Don't throw up!" Millie cautioned. "The maid's already gone for the day, and I'd have to clean it up. Sit down. Put your head between your knees."

The sudden change in temperature made Clarisse shudder. "Somebody locked me in there," she blurted out.

"Yeah, I know. They put this broom handle in the door." Millie pointed at a large push broom on the floor. "Sometimes these women can be worse than a bunch of high school jocks," said Millie, shaking her head. "Always playing practical jokes."

"It wasn't a practical joke. Somebody tried to kill me."

"Sure," Millie said.

"I could have died in there."

"One time I saved this boy's life in a swimming pool," Millie said. "The MDC police gave me a lifesaver's medal."

"Where's Newt?" Clarisse asked sharply.

"He went home. Are you okay now?"

"Was he alone?"

"You want an extra-strength Tylenol or something?"

"Just tell me if Newt left with B.J. or not!" Clarisse demanded.

"B.J.? You mean Betty Jordan? Even if my name was Betty Jordan, I wouldn't go by the initials B.J.," remarked Millie. "You think she knows what those initials stand for?"

"How long has she been coming here?"

Millie thought a brief moment. "Since last May, I think."

"How often does she show up?"

"I'm not supposed to talk about our clients."

"Of course you're not," Clarisse said, "but if you do tell me what I want to know, I promise I won't sue the spa for allowing me to be locked in the steam room and suffer physical and psychological trauma. Now, how long has Betty Jordan been coming here?"

"Since May. She takes all her classes from Newt. She comes in twice a week just to use—" Millie's voice halted.

"The steam room?"

Millie nodded slowly.

"Would I be too far off guessing this is one of her steam days?"

"Yes, but—" Millie began, confused.

Clarisse walked away from her toward the locker room. "Thanks for saving my life," Clarisse tossed back over her shoulder.

chapter
seventeen

AT NINE-THIRTY THAT EVENING CLARISSE SWEPT INTO Valentine's office above the barroom, banged the door shut behind her, and announced, "Somebody tried to kill me this afternoon—I think."

Valentine glanced up from his newspaper. "Who is somebody, and did they or didn't they?"

Clarisse threw herself into one of the two wingback chairs facing the desk. She crossed her legs, rearranged her skirt, and folded her arms. Sitting in his swivel chair, Valentine was framed by the two-way mirror overlooking the barroom.

" 'Somebody' is B.J. I think she had some help doing it." Clarisse paused, took a breath, and then said reluctantly, "Newt . . ."

Valentine raised his eyebrows in surprise.

Clarisse detailed for him her visit to the Universal Women's Health Spa.

"After it happened, I came directly back here to tell you, but when you weren't here, I decided to have a nice quiet dinner at the Club Café and think things over. Where have you been all day, anyway?''

"Maybe it *was* just a practical joke, like the receptionist said.''

"It was no joke, Val. I told you, B.J. was eavesdropping outside the door when I was talking to Newt.''

Valentine put his newspaper aside. "So obviously you're thinking B.J. killed Ruder and Cruder? Clarisse, she may be strong, but could she kill two men, both of them bigger than her?''

Clarisse shrugged uneasily. "Newt and B.J. were together the night of the murder. The building where Ruder and Cruder were killed is only a block away from Newt's apartment.''

"We've established that. Have you done any work on motive?''

"Not yet,'' Clarisse admitted. "But remember, Newt knew other necktie victims. Jed. He had a date with All-American Boy. He knew the Shrimp, too.''

"I knew all those people, too; at least by sight. So did Niobe, and Sean.''

Clarisse leaned forward. "What earthly reason would Newt have to be so defensive about B.J. when I questioned him about her?''

"How would you react if someone asked you specific questions about the last time you had sex?''

"Okay,'' Clarisse conceded, "you have a point, but Newt has never been one for discretion, especially as far as his sexual exploits go. Also, I'd like to find out just how well those two knew each other. Now, Newt told us he'd talked to B.J. in the bar a few times, but the receptionist told me she's been going to the spa for months.''

"Maybe Newt didn't talk to her at the spa for a long time. She may have been going there for months, but how long has she been taking classes from Newt?''

Clarisse paused a moment before replying. "I think Newt still has some questions to answer. I think we should talk to him, and to B.J. If they won't give us what we want, we'll go to the police.''

"I love how you so casually interchange 'I' and 'we'," Valentine remarked dryly.

"You are going to help, aren't you?"

"Yes, of course, but you realize that if we're wrong, Newt will never speak to us again, and Niobe will quit her job."

"I'll feel worse if somebody else gets murdered and you and I haven't done anything to prevent it."

"Who do we grill first? Newt or B.J.?" Valentine asked.

"Newt," Clarisse said without hesitation, "just because he's closer. B.J. lives in Cambridge, near Porter Square—I looked it up in the telephone book."

Valentine picked up the telephone receiver and punched the intercom button connecting to the bar. He swung about in his chair to look through the two-way glass at Sean answering the phone next to the cash register.

"Sean, something's come up, and Clarisse and I have to go out for a while. Would you mind working a little double-time until we get back? We shouldn't be more than a couple of hours."

Sean glanced up toward the window and nodded agreement to Valentine's request.

"For Niobe's sake," Valentine said as he hung up the telephone, "I hope our suspicions are wrong."

"You never did tell me what you were up to today," said Clarisse.

"Same thing you were—snooping around in things that didn't concern me."

"Really?" Clarisse asked in a delighted voice as they left the office. "Where did you go? What did you find out?"

Valentine locked the office door behind them. "Remember Newt's leather wristband, the one that just happened to slip off his arm and fall in the hibachi yesterday?"

"The one the carpenter *supposedly* found."

They moved down the stairwell.

"I decided to talk to his carpenter friend myself," Valentine said. "I went to that building today. I pretended I

146

was interested in buying one of the condos. I got them to let me look around. I found the carpenter Newt knows."

"And—" Clarisse urged anxiously.

"The carpenter didn't know anything about it. He said he hadn't given anything to Newt."

"Do you think the carpenter was telling the truth?"

"He had no reason to lie."

"Then why would Newt make up a story like that?"

"Good question." They reached the first floor, and Valentine followed Clarisse out to the street. The evening was warm and windless, and the last vestiges of twilight showed in a deep indigo sky free of clouds. They decided to walk to Beacon Street, a quarter of an hour away.

When they got there, they saw that Newt's apartment windows were lighted, but he didn't answer his intercom when they pressed the buzzer.

"Want to try Niobe?" Valentine asked.

Clarisse nodded and pressed Niobe's bell. "We're here to see Newt," Clarisse declared when Niobe responded, "but he's not answering."

"I'm not his secretary," Niobe answered sharply. "I'm not his doorman. He's home. Ring longer."

They rang twice again, then buzzed Niobe again, who unlatched the door without speaking.

As they mounted the stairs, Valentine and Clarisse found Niobe beating on Newt's door and shouting, "Turn that stereo off, you lying two-faced sneak!"

Loud rock music issued from Newt's apartment.

"You're sure he's here?" Clarisse asked.

"Who else in the building would play a record five times straight through at top volume? He always bangs the door shut when he goes out, and he hasn't gone out." She fished a key out of her pocket. "He doesn't know I have a key. He changed the locks when I moved out, but I bribed the locksmith. Just in case I ever have to gather evidence for our divorce case."

She pressed the key in the lock, turned it, and pushed open the door.

The hallway door opened on to the long living room of

the apartment. The dim room glowed with the failing light of the sky over the Charles. Newt sat motionless on the couch, staring toward the back windows overlooking the river.

Niobe, in a long breath of imprecations against Newt's rudeness, marched across the carpet and pushed the stylus gratingly across the turntable. Newt did not protest. In the sudden silence, Clarisse flicked on the light. Then they were able to see the dark silk necktie wound tightly about his neck and Newt's glassy, sightless stare.

part 4

labor day

chapter
eighteen

"Okay," Valentine said as he pushed the door all the way open, "what's the crisis *this* time?" He stepped over the threshold onto the gravelly surface of the roof of Slate.

Clarisse sat, arms folded, on the low brick wall dividing Slate's roof from that of the adjoining building. She wore a dove-gray sweatshirt with pushed-up sleeves, a pair of blue jeans, and dark gray Adidas running shoes. Her hair was covered with a red bandanna. She was staring toward Boston's Back Bay. It was past six o'clock, and the days at the end of summer were noticeably shortening. The lowering sun reflected blindingly off the dark glass walls of Hancock Tower.

Clarisse said nothing when Valentine came over and sat down beside her.

"You called me up here so you could give me the silent treatment?" he asked.

"I've been cleaning my apartment," Clarisse said, still not looking at him.

"Uh-oh," Valentine said darkly, "that means you've

been thinking. I remember that just before you decided to change careers you cleaned your old apartment on Beacon for a whole weekend. It was nearly as bad as the time that airline pilot asked you to marry him.''

"Cleaning clears my mind," Clarisse said. "I've been thinking about this place." She unwrapped her arms and waved one of them about.

"The roof?"

"No, idiot. Slate. Our lives here."

Valentine leaned aside and wiped away a handful of loose mortar from under him. "Oh?"

"I was thinking that we were in trouble. That maybe I'll have to drop out of law school and go back to real estate and you'll have to go to work for somebody else again. As soon as Niobe gets back, you know, Sean is quitting. He says he can't bring in decent tips here anymore."

Niobe had been in Hawaii for more than six weeks, "working out her grief," as she put it.

"Sean gave me his notice yesterday," Valentine told her. "He didn't say, but I think he got a job down the street at Fritz. I don't think Niobe will stay, either. In fact, I think she's coming back to Boston just long enough to pack up and move. I don't blame either of them. They've been loyal to us and to Slate, but they can obviously make more money somewhere else. I take it you spent the afternoon slinging Ajax and Endust and entertaining visions of the poor house."

"More or less."

"Remember, though, it's the August slump."

"Is that like the July slump we experienced?"

"Things'll pick up in September when everybody comes back to school. I *know* they'll pick up when they catch the necktie murderer."

"Nobody's died in the past six weeks," Clarisse said. "That's something."

"Nobody we know of," Valentine amended.

"We'd have heard," Clarisse said. "But no matter if the killer has stopped or not, our customers have *not* returned. I'll bet they just got out of the habit of coming to

Slate. We've been in business less than a year, and we put so much money into it . . ."

"So," Valentine said with a sigh, "when you were downstairs scrubbing the lineoleum, did you give any thought to the murders?"

"Yes," replied Clarisse seriously, "I was thinking about Newt. His death has really bothered me, because he's the one I knew best."

"He was fully clothed, and unlike all the other victims, Newt was killed in late afternoon instead of the middle of the night. Do you think a copycat killer got to him?" Clarisse nodded, and Valentine went on: "Then it was probably someone he knew and let into the building, or it was somebody who was already inside waiting for him when he got home. You think?"

"Yes, and I'll bet either way it was a woman. Suspect number one: Niobe Feng," replied Clarisse firmly. She couldn't read Valentine's expression but felt he was probably skeptical. "Well, she *was* at home all afternoon and that evening," she emphasized. "She could have gone down to talk to him and they got into one of their fights. Who would hear it? All the neighbors were at work. Niobe overpowered him in a fit of passion, and that was the end of Newt. Just as she was finishing him off, his door buzzer sounded. Niobe fled in a panic back to her place. We rang, and she let us in. The three of us went to Newt's apartment to find out why he wasn't answering his bell or the door, and there he was. What do you think?"

"Are you saying that Niobe committed the other murders?"

Clarisse frowned. "Perhaps—out of jealousy. Newt had gone to bed with Jed, also with the Shrimp, and we know he had a date with All-American Boy. All those men are dead."

"But Niobe *wasn't* jealous of the men Newt went to bed with. She only got upset when she discovered that Newt had gone to bed with B.J."

"Which brings us to suspect number two," Clarisse said.

"Convince me."

"Newt was killed on the same day I questioned him at the health spa and the same day B.J. tried to steam me to death—"

"What if it wasn't either one of them, but just some strange person's idea of a practical joke?"

"It doesn't matter. What does matter is that they left the spa together. Maybe they went back to Newt's apartment."

"Then B.J. killed him?"

Clarisse left the wall and paced about on the gravel, thinking. "Together they were the necktie murderer!" A jumbo jet rose suddenly above the downtown skyline. The roar of the engines was deafening, but when the noise subsided, Clarisse turned back to Valentine. "They did the killings together, taking separate victims. Somehow one initiated the other into it. At the spa, B.J. thought I was onto them and tried to kill me. They went to Newt's apartment to talk it over. Maybe Newt was getting paranoid. B.J. thought he was going to blow their cover, and she killed him. The woman's no slouch. She's got a good body under all that leather, and we know she's been working out."

"What about motive—sexual thrills?"

"Yes. That and cover-up," said Clarisse. "The earlier killings were the kicks. Ruder and Cruder were probably just cover-up, just as Newt was cover-up. Trying to get rid of me was an attempted cover-up."

Valentine thought this through for a few moments and then said, "Do you notice a slight difficulty with these two suspects?"

"No," said Clarisse definitely. "I'm voting for B.J."

"We're talking about a string of murders of homosexual men, but your two major suspects are heterosexual women. Doesn't that strike you as a mite improbable—not to mention that now you've got more cover-up crimes than original murders?"

"I don't think it's improbable," said Clarisse, but uncertainly. She brightened suddenly, "There's something else! How long has it been since the last murder?"

"Newt died on July fifth," said Valentine. "No murders since then."

"Niobe's been out of town since Newt's funeral," Clarisse pointed out.

"What about B.J.?"

"B.J.'s been in Provincetown. She'll be back Labor Day weekend. I did my homework—"

She broke off as she glanced toward the Warren Avenue side of the building and moved closer to the edge.

Curious as to what had drawn her attention, Valentine joined her and saw a Boston Gas repair truck just rounding the corner from Berkeley Street.

"Did you know that Bander was seeing Sean again?" Clarisse asked suddenly.

"No," said Valentine, genuinely surprised. "Is this rumor or fact?"

"Sean told me. He wouldn't tell you because you've made it abundantly clear what you think of Bander."

"How long have they been seeing each other?"

Clarisse thought for a moment. "He didn't say exactly, but I got the impression it's been a while. Over a month, at least." Then her brow wrinkled. "That means that Bander has been out of circulation for a while, too—just like Niobe and B.J."

"Clarisse, please tell me you don't have this theory about the necktie killer being an unhappy and unpleasant homosexual Boston Gas repairman desperately looking for a lover but everytime he falls for someone they reject him and he strangles them. Please say that's not what you're thinking."

"Well . . ." Clarisse hedged. "Something like that. Anyway, who said murder couldn't be romantic?"

Valentine rolled his eyes. "So why aren't we accusing Father McKimmon?"

"Father McKimmon?"

"That's right, Lovelace. I haven't seen him once since July."

"Oh, God." Clarisse sighed. "I'd forgotten all about

Father McKimmon. He knew Newt, and he knew Jed and the Shrimp and . . ."

"Do you think this roof is wired?" Valentine asked suddenly.

"Wired?"

"You know—bugged. State-of-the-art listening devices disguised as gravel or something."

Clarisse turned and looked up at the moon, visible this late afternoon. "It's not even a first-quarter moon yet and already you're acting strange."

Valentine leaned slightly forward. "Look down at the police station. Third floor left window. There're two of them with binoculars, and they sure aren't star gazing."

"Oh, them," Clarisse said calmly. "They've been there since I came up here a while ago. You know, I think they probably suspect that you and I committed all those murders."

Valentine looked directly into the window of the police station, and bared his teeth in a broad grin.

chapter
nineteen

"OH, MY GOD, VALENTINE!" CLARISSE SCREECHED AS SHE clambered up onto the car seat and squeezed herself though the open skylight of the rented Thunderbird. "It's beautiful here!"

"Positively bucolic," Valentine replied unenthusiastically as his eyes swept across the thick forest surrounding River Pines Lodge. He let go of the steering wheel and turned off the ignition.

"Your heels are going to rip the fabric," he called up to her. "I didn't take vandalism coverage on this thing, remember?"

Clarisse lowered herself and settled back into the seat. She adjusted her wide-brimmed tan straw hat and picked at the bow of the pink ribbon securing it under her chin. She tossed the trailing ribbon ends over her shoulders, pushed her large octagonal dark glasses up on the bridge of her nose, and looked at Valentine.

"Val, I'm well aware of your dislike of a landscape minus a view of a distant city skyline, but I do not want to hear it today. I *need* a day in the country." She breathed contentedly and then leaned over to catch sight of herself in the rearview mirror. "How do I look?"

Valentine pressed back against his door to avoid a slashing with the edge of her straw hat. He observed her briefly. She also wore a white blouse with short puffed sleeves and pink cuffed and pleated Forties-style shorts.

"You look like you're in drag as Katharine Hepburn."

"Is Katharine Hepburn *still* alive?" a garbled female voice rasped from behind them.

Valentine and Clarisse both turned as Niobe rose blearily from the backseat where she had been sleeping since they left Boston two hours earlier.

"How do you feel?" Clarisse asked.

Niobe sat all the way up and yawned loudly as she rubbed her eyes. When she dropped her hands into her lap, her eyes were still closed. "I still have jet lag. What was that squealing about a minute ago? Did we run over a pig?" She yawned again.

"We've arrived, Niobe. We're here at River Pines, and it's lovely."

Niobe raised one eyelid. She turned her head slightly and then opened the other eye. "Oh, God, we're in the woods!" she shrieked. "How did we end up here? Do we have any food? Are we going to starve?"

Clarisse shifted back around. "This is River Pines Lodge. Remember? Labor Day Weekend? Bartenders' Weekend? All your old friends from around New England and New York? A smart barbecue followed by a smart tubing contest?"

Niobe threw herself forward and grabbed Valentine's shoulder. "I said I'd go out for drinks with you two. I *didn't* say I wanted to be dragged to the end of the earth for them! I hate trees, *especially* ones with pine needles and leaves on them! How did this happen to me?"

"I asked you last night after you got back. You said 'yes.' That's how."

"You took advantage of my jet lag. Fresh air makes me nauseous."

"Come on, Niobe," Clarisse persisted. "We'll be back

in Boston by midnight and, for all I care, you can inhale fumes directly from the exhaust pipe of a Greyhound bus. Right now though, all three of us are going to try to have a good time.''

''Fresh air may make you sick, Niobe,'' Valentine said over his shoulder, ''but being confined in a small space with a cheerful woman is a real killer.''

Clarisse opened the glove compartment and took out three plastic encased name tags reading ''SLATE—BOSTON'' and gave one to Valentine and another to Niobe.

Clarisse opened her door and got out of the car. ''I'm going to reacquaint myself with Mother Nature for a few hours,'' she said, pinning on her own tag.

''All I want to do is reacquaint myself with a stiff gin and tonic,'' Valentine said as he got out of his side.

''Make that two gins,'' Niobe said as she crawled out of the back seat. ''Then maybe I can handle all this green hanging around everywhere.''

The River Pines Lodge, three-storied and made of logs, lay deep in the forests of southern Vermont. From its wide, deep veranda, there was a view to the west of the Green Mountains, and to the south of a stretch of the narrow, turbulent Cold River. The forest hugged around the lodge on every side.

Clarisse proceeded Valentine and Niobe up the steps to the veranda and stopped to look down toward the sun-sparked surface of the river. She lifted her sunglasses to look about and see if she recognized any of the dozen or so men sitting in the chairs facing the small lawn. Several men were already setting up picnic tables for lunch. More cars and VW vans were pulling up. License plates read Massachusetts, Connecticut, Rhode Island, New Hampshire, Maine, Vermont, and New York.

Niobe came up onto the top step and shaded her eyes as she looked at the new arrivals. ''It's the Roadies,'' she announced.

''Who?'' Valentine asked.

''Bartenders from Rhode Island. I worked at a bar in Rhode Island once, did you know that?''

"No," Clarisse said as she looked past Niobe and waved to several men emerging from inside the Lodge. They were bartenders from the Boston Ramrod.

"Rhode Island is the next closest thing to hell on earth," Niobe announced loudly—within hearing of the arrivals from that state.

"Oh?" Valentine asked, "What's the *closest* thing to hell on earth?"

"Waking up in a forest stone sober."

Valentine pulled open the screen door. "The bar's across the room." He nodded toward the cool interior of the massive lodge living room—one long undivided space filled with comfortable couches, rag rugs, and a ratty moosehead over the fireplace.

Niobe fled inside. Valentine and Clarisse followed her just over the threshold of the lodge but Clarisse caught Valentine's wrist. "Val, that woman down at the other end of the room—does she seem familiar to you?"

"Yes. She looks very much like Elvis Presley after he got on drugs."

"Not her. The woman with curly blonde hair and sunglasses in the jeans and cowboy shirt, talking with the two men in the green t-shirts."

"No, don't recognize her. I do know the two numbers she's talking to, though. The muscular ones with the mustaches are Fred and Mike. Fred's the one with wavy hair and Mike's the short hair. They own River Pines."

"They don't have nicknames, I hope—like Frick and Frack or something, do they?"

'Nope. Why?"

"After Ruder and Cruder, and The Ice Maiden, I never know what to expec—wait! *That's* who the woman is! It's B.J.!"

Valentine peered at the blonde woman. "Are you sure?"

"Yes," said Clarisse definitely. "Take a good look. She's cut her hair, and she's not wearing her black leather."

"So it is B.J.," Valentine said. "I wonder why she isn't in her leather?'

"Maybe she's going tubing later. It would be difficult

floating downriver in a tire if you're weighted down with whips and chains. I wonder who she came with? Anyway, I'm glad she's here. One of us can talk with her, and then we'll see how right or wrong our suspicions are."

"I was sort of hoping in all this back-to-nature business you'd forgotten about snooping for a little while."

Clarisse fussed with the ribbon of her large hat. "Val, I am perfectly capable of sniffing flowers while looking for a snake in the underbrush."

Valentine rolled his eyes. "Oh, brother."

"Well, well, the gang's all here."

Clarisse and Valentine were both startled by the deep voice and turned quickly. Press was coming down the staircase that led to the guest rooms on the second and third floors. Charcoal sketching pencils rested behind each of his ears, and he had a medium-sized sketch pad tucked under his arm.

"And Niobe, too?" Press asked, glancing into the bar. "Who's minding the store?"

"I decided to adhere to the true spirit of this holiday," Valentine said, "and close Slate for the day. A miniholiday for manager and staff."

Press raked platinum hair off his forehead with one hand and barely suppressed a smirk. "Rumor speaketh otherwise . . ."

"Rumor usually speaketh with a forked tongue," Clarisse said darkly. "What's it saying this time?"

"Not much, really," Press admitted.

A group of men came through the front door and, as Valentine knew them from past Bartenders' Weekends, there were brief greetings.

"Just what is 'not much'?" Clarisse persisted, *"Really?"*

Press pulled one of his charcoal pencils from behind an ear and flitted it through his fingers as he talked. "I just heard that Slate has closed its doors for the last time. That it's going to reopen as a straight bar called 'South Endie Trendies.' That the two of you have lost your financial shirts but that you didn't care because the whole thing was a tax write-off anyway.''

"When did you first hear this rumor?" Valentine demanded.

"Oh, about two and a half seconds after you pulled in the parking lot," Press replied, smirking again.

"It's not true," Clarisse snapped.

"Rumors fly when you're having a good time." Press shrugged. He pushed his hair back again, nodded curtly to Valentine and Clarisse, and then walked outside to the veranda.

"I don't think there's a rumor at all," Clarisse said. "I think he just made that up."

"So do I," Valentine agreed. "But it doesn't matter if he made it up or not, because he'll spread it. That's one of the wonderful things about operating a gay business—the moral support you get from the community. Let's find Niobe and help her make a dent in Fred and Mike's liquor supply."

"Get me something," said Clarisse. "I don't want to fight that crowd."

Valentine returned a few moments later with a scotch and water for Clarisse. She was standing at one of the large low windows that opened on to the veranda. "I just saw something interesting," she said.

"What?"

"As soon as Press left, B.J. went outside, too, and caught up with him. The two of them walked down to the river together. I didn't know they knew each other. What if B.J. was at Press's place the night Jed was killed?"

"I knew that was what you were going to say. What are you suggesting—that Press and B.J. are sleeping together? I can understand Newt carrying on with her, but let's face it. Press is a card-carrying homo and wouldn't change for anything."

"No," said Clarisse. "No sex. But remember, Press is an artist, and B.J. is an archaeologist. She has to have a strong background in art, so that would provide them with some common ground."

"Jed never mentioned B.J. being at their apartment."

"Maybe Jed didn't know," Clarisse argued. "Jed and Press were on the outs before Jed was killed. Press told us he and Jed left notes instead of facing each other."

"Go on," Valentine conceded.

Clarisse turned away from the windows and leaned against the sill. She removed her dark glasses and said, "Press and Jed both were out at bars the night Jed was killed. Press went to the Loft and didn't leave there until six in the morning, when the place closes. Maybe B.J. was also at the Loft that night. Press could have invited her back to his apartment. Once they got there, they got more stoned than they already were, and Press passed out. Jed, who was already home, got up later and found B.J. still there. They had words; she overpowered him, strangled him, and then left. Press slept through it all."

"There were no signs of a fight in that apartment."

"Aha," Clarisse said, waving an index finger, "I've thought of that. She could have crept into Jed's room and killed him while he slept."

"Jed would have put up a struggle," Valentine insisted, "and there was no sign of one."

Clarisse bit her lower lip. "Then she used something to overpower him—something that doesn't leave marks."

"Clarisse," Valentine said patiently, "think about this: why would B.J. kill Jed when, if your theory's right, Press was right there? He wouldn't have put up a struggle if he'd passed out."

Clarisse made a pouting frown. She put her glasses back on. "I'll think about it while I go get another drink."

"While you're gone," Valentine suggested, "come up with a reason for B.J. to murder a perfect stranger."

chapter
twenty

AFTER THEY HAD DRINKS, VALENTINE AND CLARISSE WENT off separately. Valentine fell into conversation with old friends from New Haven, and Clarisse decided to explore the lodge itself. With her scotch and water she wandered into the pool room, the small back bar, and then doubled back through the dining room into the lounging area. She selected a large overstuffed chair facing the hearth and settled well down into it. She propped her feet up on an ottoman. Clarisse stared into the cold fireplace and thoughtfully sipped her drink. Music and snatches of conversation filtered into the room from the bar and through the open windows. She felt pleasantly weary and closed her eyes.

They flew open again when rapid footfalls crossed the carpet behind her chair. Chair cushions sighed as someone sat down. This was immediately followed by a steady dull tapping of shoe against carpet. The pillows sighed again. Clarisse shifted her eyes to her left as the footfalls rushed across the carpet and there was another groan of upholstery as this restless person resumed nervous foot tapping.

"If you don't stop that," Clarisse said through clenched teeth, "I'm going to epoxy your feet to the floor."

"Who's that?" a male voice exclaimed in surprise.

Clarisse dragged her feet off the ottoman and turned. Her eyes widened as she looked over the rim of her glasses. "Well, it must be old home week."

"What are *you* doing here?" Father McKimmon asked with apparent shock. He was not wearing his priest garb, but a flowered sport shirt and tan slacks with a pair of brown deck shoes.

"Good question," Clarisse replied. "I was just about to ask it."

Father McKimmon released a deep breath. He leaned far back, his hands gripping the arms of the chair. He appeared to be forcing himself to relax. The fingers of his right hand tapped out a nervous staccato against the upholstery. "I wasn't expecting to run into a crowd here today."

"What were you expecting to run into?" Clarisse asked the priest.

Raucous laughter erupted outside the open window at Father McKimmon's back. He flinched at the sound, then took another deep, steadying breath and addressed Clarisse again. "I was told people came here to relax and not carry on. I heard the place was . . ." He frowned for want of the right word.

"Discreet?" Clarisse put in. "Most of the time it probably is, but this is a holiday weekend, you know."

Father McKimmon creased his brows. "Holi—? Oh, yes, that's right, Labor Day. Well, I don't pay attention to *those* holidays. If I had known that all these people were going to be here . . . A friend dropped me off, so I guess I'm stuck here . . . I . . ."

Clarisse wondered why the priest was so distracted. Upset at being seen at a gay resort? That didn't make sense, because he'd seen Clarisse often enough at Slate. If he'd never admitted that he was gay, he'd at least never denied that he enjoyed the company of gay men.

Clarisse removed her dark glasses. "Your retreat is somewhere in this area, didn't you tell me?"

"Yes," said McKimmon eagerly. "Yes, it's about ten miles from here. Very close, in fact. And quite frequently this summer I came over here . . ." He faded out again.

"To get away from things," Clarisse suggested, but she knew that *to get sloshed* was probably much nearer the mark.

"Yes," McKimmon said, "to get away from things."

"It was terrible about Newt, wasn't it?" Clarisse said suddenly.

"Newt?"

"Ricky Newton."

"Oh, yes, Niobe's husband. Terrible."

Clarisse looked surprised. "I was told he used to be a student of yours."

McKimmon pulled up short. "I've had so many over the years. But of course I remember him from the bar. Yes, it was dreadful how he ended up."

"Were you in town when it happened?" Clarisse asked innocently.

"I don't know."

Clarisse raised an eyebrow. "It was July fifth."

McKimmon bit at his lower lip. "The middle of the summer was a rough time for me, I'm afraid. I don't actually have much memory of *what* was going on at that time."

"You must remember what you did on July Fourth. That wasn't even six weeks ago."

"I celebrated," said McKimmon curtly, and got up out of the chair. "Is Niobe here?"

"She's at the bar, I think," Clarisse said.

"I have to give her my condolences," said the priest, and walked out of the room before Clarisse had the opportunity to ask him anything else.

IN THE MEANTIME, VALENTINE HAD REMOVED HIS SHIRT and was deep into a game of volleyball, which had begun as soon as all the bartenders had taken a vote on whether this was to be a competitive or noncompetitive match.

"Cutthroat" was ventured as a third option and won. Sean was on Valentine's team, just ahead of him in rotation. Several times in the course of the game Valentine had to call Sean's attention back to the game. Sean appeared less interested in winning than in watching Press, who sat sketching the players, his back against the trunk of an oak.

Once, as the ball sailed over the net to Valentine's team, Sean leaped suddenly high into the air, twisted his torso to one side, and slammed his fist into the ball. It shot in an arc away from the net and slammed into the oak tree, just inches from Press's head.

"Sean," Valentine said, mystified by the man's action, "What's wrong with you?"

Without missing a beat, Press got to his feet and said aloud, "Sean doesn't like witnesses; that's what's wrong with him." He ambled away into the thick forest.

One of the opponents retrieved the ball. The game immediately resumed.

The volleyball game went on for another twenty minutes, with a victory for the team opposing Valentine. The players dispersed, most returning to the coolness of the barroom and others stripping to their swim trunks and racing toward the shore of Cold River. Valentine remained by the net and wiped sweat from his body with his wadded up T-shirt. Press reemerged from the forest on his way to the river.

"Let's see," Valentine called to him, indicating the sketchbook.

"Don't drip," Press demanded as he opened the book and flipped the pages for Valentine's inspection. He saw quick sketches of the volleyball game, of men sitting in rockers on the porch, and one of Niobe at the bar inside the lodge.

"Who's that?" said Valentine, pointing at one of the last sketches, less detailed than the others.

"I thought it was a pretty good likeness."

"It looks like Bander," said Valentine.

"It is."

"Is he here today?"

Press grinned maliciously. "That's what Sean's little outburst was about. That's how some people react after they've been bitten by the green-eyed monster."

"Sean's jealous of *you*?"

"Not only jealous but mad as hell."

"Do I have to play Twenty Questions just to get a simple answer?"

Press looked up—he'd been filling in one of the sketches. "Oh, all right, it's not very interesting, anyway. Sean was seeing Bander—whom I take it you know—"

"What do you mean 'was seeing'? I just heard on Wednesday that they were back together again."

"Like the song says, 'What a Difference a Day Makes,' or in this case, a phone call."

"I hate mystic utterances, Press."

"Sean's pissed at me because this morning he showed up at Bander's apartment and I was there. They had a row and a half. They threw each other around a little, and then Sean stormed out." Press took a breath. "Then Bander and *I* had a row."

"About what?"

"About the fact that he'd deliberately arranged that little scene—using me as the third party. When we got up this morning, I went to take a shower. He went to make coffee. The kitchen and bath are right next to each other. He called Sean and told him to come on over. I didn't tell him I'd heard him call, but I rushed like hell to get out of there. I wasn't fast enough, and suddenly there was Sean."

"Why would Bander do a lousy thing like that?"

"Like what? Sleep with me or purposely sabotage a relationship?"

"Screw their relationship, of course." Valentine looked away and back. "Sean must be pretty upset."

"I don't know what his story is. And tell you the truth, I don't care. Bander's one pretty strange cookie so far as I'm concerned."

"Why?"

"Let's just say that since Jed was killed I don't particularly like kinks between the sheets. In fact, I haven't even thought about sex much. I only went home with Bander because he was the best-looking man in the Eagle last night. He was also the only one who looked even remotely approachable."

"What did Bander want to do?"

"No details," Press said adamantly, "but I don't like bondage, discipline, or verbal abuse. I got enough of that working as a floorman in Filene's B."

"But you did stay the night with him."

"I wouldn't let him take his toys out, and I made him keep his mouth shut, figuratively speaking. Ask Sean if you want to know sordid details; just don't bring my name up unless you want to see how high you can raise his blood pressure. Now, I made a promise to myself to fill the sketchbook by the end of the day, and I've got a dozen blank pages, so I'm moving on to bigger and better things."

"Just one more ques—"

"No more anything," Press said, and turned on his heel, walking quickly away in the direction of the riverbank.

CLARISSE HAD FALLEN ASLEEP FOR A QUARTER OF AN HOUR inside the lodge and woke up refreshed. She had her scotch and water refilled and then wandered outside, down to where Fred and Mike were supervising the lunch setup in a willow-surrounded clearing at the margin of the tumbling Cold River. She stepped over and around gossiping sun worshippers sprawled out all over the lawn until she was at the very edge of the stream. The sun was very bright on the water. Even with her sunglasses Clarisse had to shade her eyes with a hand for a clear view of the swimmers. A squeal of laughter rose sharply behind her and grew louder. Someone thumped hard against her, and Clarisse stumbled awkwardly to one side, her hat flopping down across her eyes and temporarily blinding her. She deftly regained her footing, but not before sloshing half her drink across her blouse and onto the oiled backs of several sunbathers, who yelped at the unexpected coldness on their skin.

Angrily, Clarisse yanked up the brim of her hat and

whirled about with harsh words ready for whoever had so rudely pummeled her.

"Sorry," B.J. exclaimed with exaggerated insincerity as she ran off the short wooden pier into the water. Her jeans and cowboy shirt had been replaced by only a scanty bikini bottom. B.J. belly-flopped in the water, and Clarisse was showered with the results of her impact. B.J. squealed again, and without warning leaped up onto the back of the woman Valentine had said resembled a besotted Elvis Presley.

Clarisse glared at B.J.'s bare back. She leaned over and apologized to the disgruntled men she'd splashed. She was about to leave when a hand gripped her ankle. Clarisse revived her glare and looked down to see Bander. He was dressed only in a bright red, wide-banded jockstrap. His gray Boston Gas uniform was folded into a pillow beneath his head.

"You're all wet, Lovelace," he said, and laughed softly as he released her leg.

Clarisse smiled sweetly and upended her glass. The remainder of the iced scotch and water cascaded over the man's face and shoulders.

"So are you, Bander," Clarisse replied.

Several men hooted, and Clarisse waved graciously to them as she made her way back toward the lodge, brandishing her empty glass above her head like a trophy.

chapter
twenty-one

LUNCH WAS SERVED AT A QUARTER PAST TWELVE. VALENtine and Clarisse tried to talk to one another across paper plates, exchanging what they'd heard and what they'd speculated, but there were interruptions on every side.

"We'll talk in the car," Valentine said, pouring coffee out of an urn for them both, "on the way back to Boston."

"No good," said Clarisse. "We're hauling Niobe back with us, remember?"

At one-fifteen, Fred stood on the front steps of the lodge and held an electronic bullhorn to his mouth: "The tubing contest will begin at one-thirty sharp! Contestants please assemble in the parking lot to claim their tires!"

The crowd abandoned its beer or coffee and moved toward the bare dirt lot where the cars and vans were parked. There, at the edge of Cold River, nearly a hundred truck-tire inner tubes were neatly stacked. Mike and a helper were checking them for buoyancy and adding air to those that seemed slack.

"Sure you won't change your mind and come along?"

Valentine asked Clarisse. "Probably the last opportunity of the season to tube the Cold River."

"Valentine, I'd rather be strapped to a maharajah's widow committing suttee than be seen floating spreadeagled down a stream in a rubber tire. Besides," Clarisse added breezily, fluffing the bow of her hat ribbon, "I'm not dressed for it."

"What are you going to do for the next couple of hours? Nobody'll be back till four at least."

"First I'm going to inventory the liquor supply, and then I'm going to run a safety check on the hammocks."

"Contestants, claim your tires and entry numbers!" Fred's bullhorned voice demanded.

"Clarisse, I don't think tubing is Press's sort of activity, either," Valentine said quietly. "If you run into him, find out everything you can about Sean and Bander breaking up."

"They broke up?" Clarisse squeaked. "Niobe told us just a few hours ago they were back together again."

Valentine shrugged. "Life moves too fast for me nowadays." He winked and then broke into a jog toward the parking lot.

All one hundred inner tubes were dragged and carried down to the river. The contestants tied on their assigned luminous orange-and-black number flags and then proceeded to toss their tubes into the water and waded out to acclimate themselves to the frigid temperature of the mountain stream. Clarisse moved down to watch and waved back to anyone who waved to her first. The Cold River was just deep enough to make navigation via inner tube safe and relatively easy. There was little danger of drowning. The contestants, paddling with arms and legs, bumped their tubes into and off others playfully in anticipation of the start of the contest. A rope, one end in Mike's hand and the other tied to a tree across the lake, marked the starting line behind which the contestants crowded.

There seemed to be much confusion among the contestants, and people kept rushing over to Fred and Mike and asking them questions. It seemed as though the start of the race would be delayed for a while, and Clarisse got tired of waiting. She walked back to the lodge but got only as far as the veranda steps before she changed direction and walked across the yard and went into the forest. She discovered a well-worn path that followed, more or less, the line of the river.

Clarisse walked along the arc of the river. Farther upstream, the tubes behind the starting rope looked like enormous black lifesavers crowding on the water. She lifted her glasses and tried to find which tube Valentine was in but was unable to spot him.

Clarisse was surprised by how suddenly she was swallowed up by the trees, the dense vegetation cutting off sight of the lodge and its guests, and very quickly their noise, as well. She could hear birds, animals rattling in the underbrush, the swift sweep of the Cold River a dozen or so yards away—but nothing else. The trees were tall here, pines and firs mostly, and provided a dense canopy of lush green. The sunlight was filtered and dim, and underneath her feet was a thick carpet of decaying needles.

She bent down to study a clump of tiny yellow flowers blooming in the crevice of a decayed stump. Then she leaned over even farther to determine if they had scent. A noise came unexpectedly behind her—dry wood snapping clean. It did not seem close by, but it was near enough to cause Clarisse to freeze and listen closely. Her peripheral vision was blocked by her hat, so she stood up and removed her dark glasses. She looked about casually as if doing no more than trying to catch a glimpse of the nearby stream. Nothing stirred. She relaxed, replaced her glasses, and moved farther along the path. The eerie feeling of being watched crept over her again.

Clarisse froze once again. She hissed in a sharp breath as she rolled her hands into fists at her side, her eyes riveted to the edge of the dirt path. A thin whitish snake was coiled in the moss in the shadow of some broken flat rocks. Clarisse bit her lower lip and held her breath. The muscles of her calves tightened, and her toes curled back in her sandals. She remembered from the sixth grade that there were four species of poisonous snakes in the continental United States but could not remember how many of those four species could be found in mixed coniferous forests of southern Vermont. She very slowly uncoiled the fingers of her right hand and raised her arm to her face, edging her glasses up with an extended finger. Suddenly her whole body relaxed, and she expelled her breath loudly in relief. She let her glasses drop back onto the bridge of her nose and then bent forward and plucked the length of white from among the leaves and held it up before her eyes. It was no snake at all, but an old rosary of intricately carved ivory beads. Though the crucifix was missing, the beads were not stained or dirty, so she guessed it had not been on the ground for very long.

Again she had the sensation of being watched, and she snapped her head about. As if on cue, leaves briefly rustled behind her. Clarisse looked all about her, without any pretense this time, but was unable to pinpoint the source of the noise. She dropped the rosary into her pocket and moved back along the path, retracing her steps.

She cried out sharply when something dark and blurred shot past her feet. She chided herself immediately when she saw that it was a squirrel. The animal stopped a few yards off the path and went up on its hind legs. It stared not at Clarisse but well past her through the trees. Clarisse knitted her brow curiously and followed the animal's line of vision. From what she could determine, the squirrel was looking in the direction of two large sycamores whose trunks had grown together and then separated into a widening V not far off the ground. Clarisse stepped off the path and made her way over to the mutant trees.

Leaning against the divided trunks and peering through the V of the sycamore Clarisse saw Bander sprawled on the ground, facedown, unmoving. His arms were extended from his sides. A red-striped necktie was wound and crossed about his neck, one end of it draped over the shoulder of his gray uniform. Clarisse rushed around the tree and dropped to her knees at his side. Finding the tie was unknotted, she yanked it from around his neck. She grabbed

174

Bander's arm and rolled him onto his back. His cheek and nose knocked against her knee. His lips parted, and he emitted a deep, guttural moan.

"Thank God . . ." Clarisse breathed. She slapped his cheek, then once again, but more firmly. "Bander . . ."

The man dragged a hoarse, involuntary breath into his lungs. His eyes came open, showing only whites. They blinked closed again, then parted to show dilated irises. "What the hell ha . . ." he asked thickly, and then coughed. He put a hand to his throat as Clarisse helped him sit up. She brushed away a few twigs and crushed leaves clinging to his uniform.

Clarisse retrieved the red striped tie and showed it to him. He took it in both his hands, stared at it, but didn't speak.

"Somebody tried to kill you," said Clarisse, "unless, of course, this was just a little auto-bondage *al fresco* that got out of hand."

Bander slowly got to his feet. Clarisse tried to help, but he pushed her away.

"Did you see who it was?" he asked.

Clarisse shook her head. "No. I think I must have scared him away."

Bander leaned into the V of the sycamore. He stretched his neck this way and that, massaging it with one hand. "Him?"

"It was a woman?"

"I don't know," said Bander, harshly clearing his throat. "I was just wandering around out here when I saw this weird-looking tree. I came over to look at it. Somebody just popped up behind me, and the next thing I know, this was around my neck, and then we were struggling, and I blacked out."

"You didn't even get a glance at who it was?" Clarisse persisted.

Bander shook his head. He closed his eyes and drew a breath to steady himself. When he opened his eyes again, he said, "If you hadn't come along . . ." Bander stopped abruptly. He slid the tie through his hands. "Maybe nobody tried to kill me at all." He looked at Clarisse. "Maybe this was just somebody's idea of a practical joke?"

"I doubt it," Clarisse replied, taken aback. "It's pretty sick for a joke, and what's practical about strangling someone until they pass out?"

"Some people get off on it."

Clarisse stared at him a moment. "Bander," she said emphatically, "I hardly have to remind you that over half a dozen men have already been murdered in Boston with no apparent motive—and everyone strangled with a necktie."

"Not everyone. The man in the Fenway bushes was strangled with his own belt." He looked at her. "The man who lived on Comm. Ave. was strangled with panty hose. Anyway, those guys were killed in Boston. This is Vermont."

Clarisse's eyes widened. "They were friends of yours?"

"Tricks, actually. Besides, I don't know *exactly* what did happen just now. And I'm certainly not going to go off half-cocked and call the cops and risk it getting into the papers and losing my job."

"That's not it at all," Clarisse challenged. "You're scared, aren't you?"

"I don't want to talk about it any more, okay?"

"No, it isn't okay, Bander. Will you at least give *some* thought to going to the police? I'll go with you to verify your story."

"All right, all right. I'll think it over. Right now I need a drink."

Bander threw the tie over one shoulder. He pushed away from the tree and headed in the direction of the lodge.

"Not one word of thanks?" Clarisse called after him.

"Thanks," he said over his shoulder.

Clarisse followed behind Bander and watched him until he went inside the lodge. She continued on to the edge of the Cold River. All the contestants were at last in their tubes, massing behind the starting rope. Clarisse scanned the men until she spotted Valentine. She called his name loudly and waved frantically with one hand to get his attention, splashing a few feet into the water.

The man in the tube turned to her lazily. He had blond hair and a darker beard—but he was not Valentine. Clarisse swore under her breath. Behind her on the shore the starting gun signaling the beginning of the race exploded, and the rope barrier was dropped into the water. All eighty-five tubes started toward her, occupants screaming their starting excitement. Alarmed, Clarisse stumbled back over some rocks beneath the water. Her glasses slipped from her face and splashed in the stream. She made a lunge to grab them and lost her footing, then her balance, and tumbled backward, landing atop a thin mustached man wearing the number twenty-three.

Twenty-Three caught her before she could do any damage to him or flip over his tire. Clarisse had fallen onto her side. Her tilted hat covered her face. She tore at it madly. The man pulled her around onto her back beside him. Clarisse's bottom plunked through the tire opening, and she felt the sudden cold of the water. Twenty-Three yanked her hat up until it was out of her face but now resting on the right side of her head, the bow adorning her left ear.

"Welcome aboard!" Twenty-Three beamed, exposing a toothy smile beneath a bushy mustache one shade of red lighter than his hair. His eyes were glassy and bloodshot.

"I'm mortified," Clarisse exclaimed as she twisted her hat back into place. "Please, just get me out of this thing."

"Hey," Twenty-Three protested, "this is a race. And we're in it for the duration."

"What?" Clarisse looked about. The shore of the stream was far away on either side of them, and dozens of other tubers turned and swirled all about.

"You should have dressed for this," Twenty-Three remarked. "You're gonna do a real number on yourself. Speaking of numbers . . ." He fished a joint out of his pocket.

"No, thank you," said Clarisse a little stiffly. "I'd just like to get out of this tire."

"No can do, matie."

"I hate it when people call me matie," Clarisse said. "Please don't do it."

Clarisse twisted about, trying to catch sight of Valentine.

"Hey," protested Twenty-Three, "stop whacking me with that hat!"

Sean floated past. "You're never going to win two to a tube," he remarked.

"She's a stowaway," Twenty-Three said.

"Sean, help me!" Clarisse pleaded.

Sean waved, spinning out of reach downstream.

"Niobe!" Clarisse shouted when she saw the Chinese woman streaming past, holding hands with men in tubes on either side of her, their tires bumping against each other on their way. The tube nearest the shore blundered against a submerged rock, and the three were whipped in a line against the shore bank. Niobe and her friends screamed in laughter as Clarisse hurtled past them and out of sight around another bend.

Clarisse pushed herself far up on her hands. "I'm going to jump and swim for it."

"Sharp rocks on the bottom," Twenty-Three warned. "Undertow. Sharks. Leeches. This is the most dangerous river in North America. Have a drink."

Clarisse scanned the water and the shore on either side. The forest was thick, and they had passed no signs of habitation. She drew her breath when she saw a male figure standing on the edge of the water, half-hidden by a cedar that had nearly toppled into the water. Although she could not distinguish his face, Clarisse recognized the brightly flowered sport shirt and pale slacks she'd seen Father Mc-Kimmon wearing earlier in the day. She turned back and settled into the tire once more. At least the water was no longer frigid against her backside.

"These tires were not built for two," Twenty-Three complained. "But it won't be so bad if we both have a drink."

"Why do you keep saying that? Where do you propose to get a drink out here?"

Twenty-Three reached into the water and tugged at a

rope tied around the inner tube. When her partner took up the slack on the rope, Clarisse discovered that the other end was attached to an unoccupied tube that had been spilling along in the water behind them. When the spare came right up to their side, she saw that three six-packs of Budweiser had been strapped to the inside of the tube, keeping cold in the river water.

"Neat, huh?" said Twenty-Three proudly.

"Let me help," Clarisse said. She pulled the three six-packs out of the spare tube and dropped them into Twenty-Three's lap.

"I'm not going to drink them all at once," he protested, but by that time Clarisse had already deftly rolled herself out into the spare. She quickly untied the rope and kicked away Twenty-Three's tire.

"Thank you very much," she said, righting her hat and arranging herself as comfortably as possible for the trip downstream.

Fifteen minutes later, Clarisse was taking up the back side of the mass of tires glutting the stream. Since she could do nothing about her predicament, she decided she would try to enjoy herself. The bright sun felt good, and a soft cooling breeze wafted across the water. She closed her eyes and abruptly opened them again as someone in another tire thunked into her side. Clarisse looked and was taken aback to see B.J., one hand holding on to her tire to keep herself alongside.

B.J. held out a small amber-colored bottle with a black top. "Hey, I'm sorry I knocked into you earlier," B.J. said.

"Why apologize now?"

"I just feel good. Come on; accept my apology and have a hit."

B.J. uncapped the bottle, clamping her thumb over the opening immediately.

Clarisse drew back. "What is that?"

"Poppers."

"Amyl nitrate? No, thank you, B.J."

B.J. shrugged and recapped the bottle. "Suit yourself. I

179

just thought it might make going over the rapids more fun for you?''

Clarisse's eyes widened slowly. "Rapids?"

"Straight ahead."

B.J. gave Clarisse's tire a kick, jetting herself away with a peal of laughter. The motion sent Clarisse's tire into a turn and caused it to pick up speed.

Hoots of feigned terror from fellow tubers swept over Clarisse as, to her utter horror, she saw those ahead of her disappear in crashes of white water and mist.

Clarisse covered her face with both hands as she was swept along to the rocky curve of the rapids.

chapter
twenty-two

"OH, GOD, VAL," CLARISSE MOANED DESOLATELY, "BY tomorrow I'm going to look like a two-legged blister. Even between my toes is sunburned. I won't be able to show myself in public for at least two weeks."

Valentine stifled a smile but was unable to keep amusement out of his voice. "Now, Lovelace, it's not that bad. You look no worse that something dredged up out of the hold of the *Andrea Doria*."

"If it wouldn't imperil my life just now," Clarisse replied tightly, "I'd knock your block off for that."

Valentine and Clarisse were driving down Route 2 on their return to Boston. It was a few minutes before eight o'clock, nearing dusk. They were alone in the car, Niobe having decided to go back to the city with the manager of a rock performance bar in Boston.

Clarisse sat on a green beach towel spread across the passenger seat. Her damp hair was pulled back into a limp ponytail at the nape of her neck. Her clothes were soaked through. The blouse was missing its left sleeve, and the right pocket hung in a flap of material. She was barefoot, and her legs and forearms were marred by fresh bruises and red abrasions. Clarisse examined her legs with a distressed expression. She uncapped a tube of medicated cream they'd purchased at a drugstore after leaving River Pines Lodge a half hour earlier.

"You can't imagine how horrible it was, Val." She smoothed a blob of the bluish cream down one calf.

"What happened to your glasses, sandals, and hat, by the way?"

She picked at the ragged shoulder of her missing sleeve but didn't bother to give the obvious answer to his question. "You went through the same course I did—but you don't look any worse for wear."

"Because I didn't go tubing, that's why—I changed my mind at the last minute."

"What?" Clarisse exclaimed. "You mean all that time I was going head over heels down that stream you were safe on shore?"

"That's right. You know, when I saw you out in the water in that tire with that man, I thought you must be drunk. Then I decided you were just being the truly fun-loving girl you really are and didn't want to miss out on any of the action."

Clarisse swiped at Valentine's shoulder. "The only reason I made a complete fool of myself out there was because I thought I might catch up with you."

"By the way, what was so important that you were willing to throw yourself into one of the major streams of North America?"

"Somebody tried to kill Bander. With a necktie."

"What the hell are you talking about? Why didn't you say something earlier?"

"I was too upset after they dragged me from the water at the end of the contest. All I could think about was how embarrassed I was and how awful I looked. Anyway, it was merely an *attempted* necktie murder."

She detailed for Valentine her earlier walk in the forest and her discovery of Bander lying by the forked sycamore.

"If you weren't tubing, where were you, anyway?" she concluded.

"I was inside the lodge, looking for you."

"Did you see Bander?" she asked.

"I did, as a matter of fact."

"What did he say?" she asked eagerly.

"He didn't say anything," Valentine said. "I didn't speak to him. He had a drink in the bar with Press. They talked for a few minutes, and then they left together. They drove away in Press's car."

"Did Bander seem upset to you?"

"Yes, he did. And after he finished talking to Press, Press looked upset, too."

Clarisse thought a moment. "I knew he was more upset than he acted after I'd found him. I knew he couldn't honestly think what happened was just someone's bizarre joke."

"Well, Bander is not about to let his guard down and show either one of us that he indeed has a human side. But that's exactly what it looked like he was doing with Press."

"Somehow I'm glad to hear that."

"Why do you think he wasn't killed?" Valentine asked after a moment.

"Because I scared away his attacker," Clarisse replied readily. "I'm sure all that rustling of bushes was him or her getting the hell out of there."

"Did Bander say what he was doing out there?"

"Wandering around, like I was."

Both were silent a long moment, thinking, and then Valentine inquired, "So, who do you think it was?"

"The question of the day." Clarisse sighed. "Everyone we even remotely suspected was at the lodge today." She hesitated a moment, then went on. "I wasn't going to mention this, but just before I found Bander, I kept having this creepy feeling that there was someone in the woods, watching me, I mean."

"Maybe it was Bander."

Clarisse shook her head. "I don't think so. You know how when you're being watched you know what direction the stare is coming from?"

"Sure."

"Well, whoever it was was in the opposite direction from where Bander was lying."

"That would mean there were four people in the woods—you, whoever was spying on you, Bander, and whoever attacked Bander."

"That's right."

"Do you think you were in danger?"

"I don't know."

"Maybe it was also just someone else out for a walk."

"And maybe it was someone whose initials are C.M."

Clarisse reached into the pocket of her shorts and pulled out the ivory-beaded rosary with the missing crucifix. She draped it over the stem of the rearview mirror.

Valentine glanced away from the highway for a moment, reaching to run the beads over his fingers.

Clarisse told where and how she'd found it. "How many bartenders do you think carry ivory rosaries on a Labor Day weekend?"

"None, of course," Valentine replied, and released the beads. "But Cornelius McKimmon certainly would have one of these."

"Exactly."

"Clarisse, do you think Father McKimmon could have attacked Bander?"

"Killer priests are not unknown in the annals of crime. If McKimmon fell off the wagon today, I wouldn't put anything past him."

"There's one thing you haven't considered. Just because you found Bender with a necktie wrapped around his neck, you immediately decided it was the elusive necktie murderer. But, Clarisse, the necktie murderer has never left a witness behind."

"What are you saying? That whoever did that to Bander was a copycat killer?"

"Bander has a lot of enemies, and someone clever might have just decided to get rid of him today and conveniently make it look like it was the necktie killer. All he would have to do is carry the weapon safely folded and tucked into a back pocket and no one would be the wiser.''

Clarisse stared out the windshield. The sky in front of them was a deep blue. The lighter, dimming sky behind was reflected in the side-view mirror. ''I don't know,'' she said, sliding down in the seat and leaning her head back. ''I'm confused, tired, sunburned, and I feel a horrible headache coming on.''

Valentine switched on the radio to a station playing jazz. Soon, lulled by the music, Clarisse fell asleep. She did not wake until the car eased to a stop in front of Slate on Warren Avenue. Valentine shook her shoulder gently to wake her.

Clarisse stretched. ''What time is it?'' she yawned.

''A little after ten.''

''Just ten? Your foot must have gotten suddenly heavy on the accelerator as soon as I nodded off. While I was asleep—did you figure out who did it?''

''No,'' Valentine said, ''but I'm not through figuring. You go on up. I think I want to go for a ride and think through a few things.''

''You just rode for two and a half hours.''

''Around the city, I mean. The car's not due in till the morning. I want to take advantage of it.''

''Fine,'' Clarisse said. She reached into the backseat and snagged her belongings. ''I'm going to go up to my apartment and lie in a cool bath with a whole box of baking soda sprinkled over me, and then it's straight to bed.''

''Summer's over,'' Valentine said quietly. ''As of tonight. This was supposed to be such a good summer for us, too, wasn't it? But it all just fell apart, didn't it?''

''It sure did,'' Clarisse concurred as she opened the door. ''Breakfast tomorrow at Annie B's? My treat.''

''You're on.''

Valentine revved the engine. Clarisse got out and closed the door. She uttered a final farewell to Valentine and then went around the car to the sidewalk. Valentine had already pulled away when Clarisse discovered that she didn't have her keys.

chapter twenty-three

VALENTINE DID NOT JUST "GO FOR A RIDE"; HE DROVE directly to Beacon Hill and parked in an illegal space on Charles Street. He walked to Mount Vernon Street and up to the building where Press still lived in the apartment where Jed Black had been murdered.

After punching the buzzer to Press's apartment for the ninth time, Valentine gave up and left the stoop. He walked back to Charles and lingered on the corner by Gary Drug Company, deciding what to do next.

Valentine pushed through the door of the drugstore and went to the pay telephone on the wall. He pulled out the telephone directory and flipped quickly through the pages. A moment later he hissed a sigh of frustration. There was no listing of Bander's address and number. Valentine shoved the directory back onto the shelf beneath the telephone. He purchased a pack of peppermint-flavored Certs, tore one out, popped it into his mouth, and left the store, returning to his car.

He yanked the fluorescent orange parking ticket from under the windshield wiper, tossed it into a nearby trash basket, and got into the car. He drove two blocks before turning off Charles Street and doubling back toward Back Bay.

"I HAD AN IDEA YOU'D SHOW UP HERE TONIGHT," SEAN said as he leaned in the open doorway of his apartment.

"Am I interrupting you?" Valentine asked as he climbed the last few steps to the landing.

"Not really. I'm just transferring some music."

Sean stepped aside, and Valentine entered the apartment. Three of the tape decks were in operation. Some tuneless song with a heavy beat played but was turned very low.

"How could you know I'd come over here?" Valentine asked. "I just decided it a little while ago."

"Intuition." Sean turned the bolt on the apartment door. "Want a beer or anything?"

"No, thanks." Valentine moved around the glass coffee table and settled onto the sofa. "You going on vacation or something?" he asked. The coffee table was covered with a rumpled pile of clothes—shirts, several pairs of blue jeans, two gray wool neck scarves, a black leather belt, a vest, and a sheaf of variously colored neckties. A green plastic garbage bag was spread open on the floor beside the table, already half full.

Sean stepped up to the table and shoved a pile of the clothing into the bag. "I decided to clean out my closet. I don't wear these things anymore, so I was going to drop them off at the Salvation Army drop box over on Tremont Street tomorrow—where the elite clump to dump."

Sean stepped over to the wall of machinery and turned up the volume of the music, then fiddled with knobs and dials as he talked with his back to Valentine.

"I guess you're here because of what happened at River Pines today," Sean said.

"Um, yes . . . I am," Valentine said uncertainly. The heel of his shoe hit against something hard just under the edge of the sofa. He leaned down to see what it was.

"You knew it was coming," said Sean.

"No, I certainly didn't—" began Valentine, then broke off. "Just a minute. What are we talking about exactly?"

"My job offer."

Valentine picked up a narrow, three-inch-long amber bottle with a black cap. It was filled with liquid, and the cap was slightly loose. He was about to say something to Sean when he grimaced and then held the bottle closer to his nose. He immediately pulled it back and coughed once.

"I was going to explain everything tomorrow." Sean took a breath. "Vision Rock Studios offered me a job."

"The video outfit?" Valentine drew his eyes away from Sean's back. Quickly and soundlessly he screwed off the bottle cap, sniffed the liquid again, again made a face, and swiftly replaced the top.

"Yep," Sean said, nodding. "They made me that offer you always hear about—the one that's too good to refuse." Sean glanced over his shoulder. Valentine closed his hand about the amber bottle of liquid to conceal it. "I guess this constitutes two weeks' notice." He went back to the tape machine.

"Niobe's going to quit, too," Valentine said distractedly.

"Going to?" Sean said too quickly, again glancing over his shoulder.

"What do you know that I don't?"

"Umm, you better talk to Niobe."

"Come on, out with it."

"Well, I'll deny I spilled the beans, but Niobe ran into the manager of Octopus at the lodge today. He offered her a job working their new dance bar. She snapped it right up. It's not like this is coming out of the blue." Sean turned back to Valentine. "I think you knew Niobe and I would probably be moving on. You pay good wages, but when the tips all but dry up . . ."

"I didn't come to see you to talk about Slate," Valentine said. "I came about Bander."

Sean hesitated. "What about him?"

"Why is it you never mentioned that you and Bander had gotten back together?"

"What difference does it make?"

"Just tell me, Sean."

"Because you two don't get along and I didn't want daily grief about my taste in lovers. Besides, my private life is just that."

"How's it working out this time?" Valentine asked blandly.

Sean didn't reply immediately. "Who have you been talking to?"

Valentine hesitated, too. Then he said, "Press."

Sean turned around to face Valentine. "Press? Just what *did* Press have to say about me?"

"He said you'd walked in this morning and found him in Bander's apartment and that Bander had set the whole thing up." Valentine tried to gauge Sean's reaction to this, but the bartender's face was blank. "Also, I saw Press leave the lodge with Bander this afternoon."

"Oh?" Sean looked confused.

"I was wondering how that made you feel—finding Bander sleeping with Press?"

"It made me feel lousy, that's how it felt, what do you think? It makes me feel pretty lousy to hear you talk about it right now. What's wrong with you, Daniel?"

"Somebody tried to kill Bander up at the lodge today."

"What?" Sean exclaimed.

Valentine leaned over and snatched one of the neckties from the pile of clothing. He held it up. "With one of these."

Sean stared at Valentine a long moment. "Who'd do that? I mean, who'd be stupid enough to kill somebody when there were people all over the place?"

"Exactly what I asked myself," Valentine said. He tossed the necktie back onto the pile. "Why are you suddenly deciding to get rid of your ties, Sean?"

"I didn't *suddenly* decide to get rid of anything," Sean replied sharply, stepping away from the revolving tapes. "Those clothes have been lying there for three days."

Valentine held his closed hand out and then opened his fingers to reveal the small bottle cradled in his palm.

Sean's brow wrinkled. "What the hell is that?"

"Is that what you used to subdue your victims?"

"What?"

"You heard me, Sean."

"This is crazy. What in hell are you accusing me of?"

Valentine stood. He moved away from the sofa, speaking rapidly but evenly as he did. "All of the murders were committed in the middle of the night, after the bars had closed. The victims were regulars at Slate, and they apparently knew their killer. Each murder took place within a half-mile radius of this building, Sean—of this apartment. The Fenway is less than fifteen minutes' walk down Marlborough Street. The building where B.J.'s two playmates were murdered is a couple of blocks in the other direction. Newt and Niobe live a block away from there. Beacon Hill's just a short distance beyond that. All-American Boy lived on the edge of the South End, just on the other side of Prudential Plaza. That makes a circle—with this apartment at the center." He looked at the bottle in his hand. "This is the real key, though. This is really what's stymied the entire Boston police force for months."

Sean stared at the bottle, then lifted his eyes to Valentine.

"You went after Bander in the forest today, didn't you? What you didn't count on was Clarisse also being in the forest, so you got the hell out of there and joined the contest just as you'd planned and nobody saw you—not even Bander."

"You son of a bitch!" Sean hissed slowly. He stepped over to Valentine, pulling his arm and fist back. He swung, but Valentine darted to one side and landed his own fist into Sean's stomach. Sean groaned but did not buckle. In a deft flash of movement he swung his leg up, twisted his torso sharply to one side, and landed the flat of his foot into Valentine's solar plexus. Valentine tumbled back over the sofa and crashed to the floor on his back. The bottle flew from his hand and rolled across the carpet. Sean threw himself astride Valentine's chest and slammed his knees down, pinning his arms to the carpet. Sean took a deep breath, leaned back and grabbed one of the discarded neckties from the floor, and then pulled himself back over Valentine.

"You asked for this, Daniel. You really did."

Sean unfurled the length of tie between his fists.

With an unexpected surge of energy, Valentine buckled his body up with such force that Sean was thrown sideways but not off of Valentine. Valentine pulled one arm free and clamped it down as hard as he could over the left side of Sean's collarbone. He dug his fingers into Sean's shoulder so hard that his knuckles whitened. Sean opened his mouth involuntarily, his body stiffened with a spasm, and then he went limp. He slid onto his side next to Valentine, eyes fanning shut. Valentine wasted no time pulling himself up to his knees. He bound Sean's wrists behind him with the necktie. From his back pocket he took his white bandanna and used it to gag Sean. He stood up, breathing hard, and looked down at his friend. Valentine ran the back of a sweaty hand across his mouth, aware now of a stinging sensation. His hand came away streaked with blood. His stomach buckled suddenly as nausea rose in his throat. Valentine choked and rushed down the hallway and swung into the bathroom. He vomited into the toilet. When he finished, he flushed, then leaned over the sink, twisting on the cold-water faucet to splash water across his face. He cupped one palm and took a drink of water. Nausea welled up again within him, and he stood to take a deep breath to steady himself. He stared unbelieving into the mirror.

Behind him stood Bander, holding a red-striped necktie stretched taut between his hands.

The tie was wound about Valentine's neck before he could turn. Both men slipped on the tile and went to the floor as Valentine grabbed at the tie binding his neck. Bander's breath was hot against his face as Valentine clenched his teeth. Guttural anger grated from Bander's throat.

"I'm going to kill you," Bander rasped.

Valentine got two fingers beneath the cloth.

"Just like I killed the others," Bander whispered.

Making a fist with one hand, Valentine brought it down

like a hammer into Bander's groin. Bander yelped in agony. The tie loosened as he doubled forward. Valentine seized the edge of the sink and pulled himself to his feet. Bander grabbed Valentine's ankle, and he plummeted over Bander's prostrate body into the hallway, going down on one knee. In a flash, Bander was atop him again. Valentine pushed to his feet, and the two struggled down the length of the hall into the living room. Bander was on his knees behind Valentine, the tie once more fast about Valentine's neck, the ends yanked taut.

"I'm going to enjoy doing it to you—"

Valentine crawled forward, but every inch of progress he made only drew the garotte tighter. He could get no breath into his lungs. Behind him, Bander rose slowly to his feet.

"—just like I enjoyed doing it to the others."

Suddenly, without warning, the tie loosened about Valentine's neck. Sean, on his back behind Bander, had raised his feet and kicked his heels back. An expression of surprise streaked Bander's face as he reeled crazily over Valentine and fell heavily into the coffee table. The glass top shattered beneath his weight. One long jagged edge of glass sliced cleanly across his throat. A jet of blood made an arc and splashed horizontally across Valentine's chest and face. Blood pulsed out of a severed artery in Bander's neck as he slumped lifelessly to the floor.

Valentine rolled over and pulled the gag out of Sean's mouth. He unbound his tied wrists.

"I just want to know," Valentine said harshly, "how we're going to convince the police that is wasn't *us* who killed Bander just now."

chapter
twenty-four

"It's all on tape," Valentine explained.

"Lucky for us," Sean replied.

"Lucky for *all* of us," Clarisse said. "Val! Stop pulling away or I'll never get this to stop bleeding." She dabbed a damp cloth against his badly scraped temple.

Valentine, Clarisse, and Sean were in Valentine's office above the Slate barroom. It was after one o'clock in the morning. Less than fifteen minutes earlier the two men had returned from police headquarters on Berkeley Street where they'd been questioned and then signed statements about what had taken place in Sean's apartment. Before they left the station, Valentine had called Clarisse to tell her briefly what had happened. She met them at the door and took them to the office, where she'd laid out medicine, bandage, and bowl to tend Valentine's wound.

Valentine rested back in his swivel desk chair while Clarisse hovered over him administering to his injury. Valentine's shirt still bore the wide, jagged stain of Bander's blood. Sean sat on the other side of the desk in one of the wingback chairs.

Clarisse was already showing the signs of the bad sunburn she had predicted for herself. Her face and arms were crimson and contrasted starkly with her white blouse and white linen slacks. Behind her on the green desk blotter was a pale blue porcelain bowl of water lightly stained with Valentine's blood, a bottle of iodine, scissors, and several lengths of cut gauze and wide adhesive tape. Clarisse dropped the cloth onto the blotter and uncapped the iodine.

"Val, take your hands away from your face," Clarisse said patiently. "This'll only sting for a minute, and the pain won't begin to compare with an attempted strangulation. Thank you. All I can say, Sean," she resumed, "is thank God you decided to record your apartment noises and that Bander didn't know you were doing it."

"That tape is the only thing between us and a manslaughter charge," Valentine said as he grimaced.

"On the other hand," Clarisse mused as she replaced the iodine cap, "I've always thought it would be quite romantic to visit someone in prison every month. Talking through wire, baking cakes, and so forth."

"You're a source of undying strength in times of adversity, do you know that, Lovelace?"

"Turn the other cheek." She folded and pressed a strip of gauze to his temple and then taped it neatly into place. "Sean, I think you ought to stay at my place tonight. I know the name of a professional cleaning crew—they specialize in homicide moppings up."

Clarisse ran her fingertips over the last piece of tape and then moved around the desk between the two men. She sat on the edge and crossed her legs.

"So, I was wrong," she admitted. "No one tried to kill Bander in the forest today?"

"No. I'm sure he saw you go into the woods and followed you, with the full intent of wanting to murder you. Something—someone," Valentine corrected himself, "scared him off that idea."

"Father McKimmon," Clarisse speculated, "who was in the woods looking for his lost rosary."

"Probably," Sean said.

"At any rate," said Valentine, "Bander changed his plan. He tried to make it look as if someone had attacked *him*. A perfect chance for him to throw us off his track. It's hardly been a secret we've been looking into these murders."

"I should have realized that," Clarisse said. "Because if someone *had* tried to strangle him, he'd have had a case of ring around the neck like yours. Also, when he got up off the ground, I brushed some twigs off his back. But there weren't any dirt or grass stains—there would have been if he'd been struggling."

Valentine nodded.

"How much do you think Father McKimmon saw of any of that?" Sean asked.

Clarisse shrugged. "My guess is that he saw enough that the cops will want to talk to him, if he isn't holed up somewhere desperately trying to induce alcoholic amnesia, which is exactly what I strongly suspect he's doing at this moment." She looked at Sean again. "I'm still not clear on why Bander was at your apartment tonight. I thought you'd never speak to him again after what he'd done with Press."

"He called and said he wanted to talk, to explain some things. He'd just gotten there a few minutes before you arrived, Val. When you called up on the intercom, Bander just said he didn't want to see you, which I didn't think was strange. He asked me to get rid of you as quick as I could, and then he went to wait in the bathroom until you did leave."

"If you knew Bander was just down the hall, why didn't you call for help when you and Val got into a fight?" Clarisse asked.

Sean shrugged. "Because it was between Daniel and me. I wasn't really going to strangle you, you know. I just wanted you to realize how stupid it was for you to suspect me."

Valentine nodded.

"God," Sean said, and rested his head back, gazing at the ceiling, "all this time Bander and I were sleeping together he was murdering people—friends of mine. All this time and I never suspected a thing. He never let his guard down once." Sean looked at Valentine. "How did he manage to get away with it for so long?"

Valentine explained for Sean Clarisse's theory regarding Bander's gas-company uniform. "How many times have you seen a man in a utility uniform—or even a fireman or a policeman, for that matter—and not given him a second glance? All you remembered was the uniform, right?"

Sean thought a moment and then nodded slowly. "Yes, that's right."

"Exactly," Clarisse said, "and when Bander killed at night, he made sure it was very late at night. That way he had not only darkness but time on his side."

"He also had a bottle of chloroform in his pocket," Valentine said, and told Clarisse how he'd discovered the bottle under the edge of Sean's sofa. "My guess is that Bander hid it there just before I buzzed the apartment."

"Chloroform?" Clarisse asked.

Valentine nodded. "He carried it in a poppers bottle."

"Really?" said Clarisse. "But just one quick hit from a bottle of chloroform wouldn't be enough to render someone completely helpless, would it?"

Valentine reached about and pulled his bandanna from his back pocket. "Not if he poured it on one of these and held it over someone's nose and mouth—the way some people do with amyl."

"Very clever," Clarisse conceded.

"It was perfect," Valentine continued. "Who knows where Bander got the chloroform? Maybe he made it himself. It can be used as a solvent, too, you know. So in case something went wrong and he got blood on his uniform, he could clean it up on the spot."

"Do you think Bander's killings were premeditated?" Clarisse asked.

"We'll never know for sure."

"Well, there must be a reason Bander stopped killing after Newt was dead."

"The heat was on after that," said Valentine. "A lot of

attention in the press. And the police have been all over for the past month or so.''

''Also,'' said Sean, ''Bander and I were together almost all the time during that period.''

Clarisse uncrossed her arms. ''Well, I'd just like to know one thing. Since B.J. is off the hook and Newt's dead— *who* tried to kill me in the steam room at the health spa?''

''Nobody can prove it, but I'd bet anything that it *was* B.J. who put the broom handle in the door, but I don't think she was trying to kill you. I think maybe it was just her and Newt trying to teach you a lesson for being so nosy.''

''What about Ruder and Cruder?'' Sean inquired.

''Aha!'' Clarisse chimed in. ''I've thought that one out. ''The night Ruder and Cruder were killed, B.J. was with Newt. When Bander ran into them, he must have realized they were on their own for once. So, he suggested they all go off to that building undergoing renovation down the street from Newt and Niobe's. He might have known about the place already—maybe he'd even worked on it, setting up the lines. Ruder and Cruder probably got excited about the prospect of carrying on with an honest-to-god repairman amid plasterboard and sawdust.''

''And apparently it was pretty exciting,'' said Valentine.

''We were really lucky tonight,'' said Sean, touching his throat.

''You certainly were,'' said Clarisse soberly, looking at Valentine. ''With Sean changing jobs and Niobe leaving also, I could have been left to run this bar single-hand-edly—reaping profits left and right, wintering in Aruba, summering in Milan . . .''

''Clarisse,'' Valentine said, ''you'd hang yourself with black crepe for the rest of your life if anything actually happened to me.''

''Depends on the designer,'' said Clarisse. She stood and straightened one sleeve of her blouse. ''You both realize, of course, that the media will go absolutely wild when they get wind of what's on that tape you gave the police. A reporter's dream, having an attempted murder, a confession by same murderer, and the breathtaking—no pun intended—accidental death of a notorious killer, all on tape. You'll be interviewed on the "Today" show. ABC will do a Movie of the Week about it. I think Faye Dunaway should play me."

"Now that Marjorie Main is dead?" Valentine asked.